RAR'

THI IDEN

Also by Elizabeth George

A Great Deliverance
Payment in Blood
Well-Schooled in Murder
A Suitable Vengeance
For the Sake of Elena
Missing Joseph
Playing for the Ashes
In the Presence of the Enemy
Deception on his Mind
In Pursuit of the Proper Sinner

The Evidence
Exposed

Elizabeth George

Hodder & Stoughton

This work first published in Great Britain in 1999
by Hodder and Stoughton
A division of Hodder Headline

A CIP catalogue record for this book is available
from the British Library

ISBN 0 340 75063 4

Typeset by Palimpsest Book Production Limited,
Polmont, Stirlingshire
Printed and bound in Great Britain by
Clays Ltd, St Ives plc

Hodder and Stoughton
A division of Hodder Headline
338 Euston Road
London NW1 3BH

For Rob and Glenda,
with love

Contents

The Evidence Exposed

The Evidence Exposed

Adele Manners gave her room one last look. The bed was made. The clothes were picked up. Nothing betrayed her.

Satisfied, she shut the door and descended the stairs to join her fellow students for breakfast. The dining hall rang with the clatter of their dishes and the clamour of their talk. As always, one voice managed to soar above the rest, shrill and determined to fix attention upon the speaker.

'Hypoglycaemia. Hy-po-gly-cae-mia. You know what that is, don't you?'

Adele wondered that anyone could avoid knowing since, in their two weeks at St Stephen's College, Noreen Tucker hadn't missed an opportunity to

expatiate upon hypoglycaemia or anything else. Seeing that she was doing so once again, Adele decided
to take her plate of scrambled eggs and sausage
to another location, but as she turned, Howard
Breen came to her side, smiled, said, 'Coming?'
and carried his own plate to where Noreen Tucker
reigned, outfitted by Laura Ashley in an ensemble
more suited to a teenager than a romance writer at
the distant end of her fifth decade.

Adele felt trapped. She liked Howard Breen. From
the first moment they had bumped into each other
and discovered they were neighbours on the second
floor of L staircase, he had been very kind to her,
preternaturally capable of reading past her facade
of calm yet at the same time willing to allow her
to keep her personal miseries to herself. That was
a rare quality in a friend. Adele valued it. So she
followed Howard.

'I'm just a martyr to hypoglycaemia,' Noreen was
asserting vigorously. 'It renders me useless. If I'm not
careful . . .'

Adele blocked out the woman's babbling by
scanning the room and engaging in a mental

recitation of the details she had learned in her two weeks as a student in the Great Houses of Britain class. *Gilded capitals on the pilasters*, she thought, *a segmented pediment above them.* She smiled wryly at the fact that she'd become a virtual encyclopedia of architectural trivia while at Cambridge University. Cram the mind full of facts that one would never use and perhaps they might crowd out the big fact that one could never face.

No, she thought. *No, I won't. Not now.* But the thought of him came to her anyway. Even though it was finished between them, even though it had been her choice, not Bob's, she couldn't be rid of him. Nor could she bury him.

She had made the decision to end their affair, putting a period to five years of anguish by coming to this summer session at St Stephen's College in the hope that an exposure to fine minds would allow her to forget the humiliation of having lived for half a decade in the fruitless expectation that a married man would leave his wife for her. Yet nothing was working to eradicate Bob from memory, and Noreen Tucker was certainly not the incarnation of razor intellect that Adele had hoped to find at Cambridge.

She gritted her teeth as Noreen went on. 'I don't know what would have happened to me if Ralph here hadn't insisted that I go to the doctor. Always weak at the knees. Always feeling faint. Blacking out on the freeway that time. On the freeway! If Ralph here hadn't grabbed the wheel . . .' When Noreen shuddered, the ribbon on her straw hat quivered in sympathy. 'So I keep my nuts and chews with me all the time. Well, Ralph here keeps them for me. Ten, three, and eight p.m. If I don't eat them right on the dot, I go positively limp. Don't I, Ralph?'

It was no surprise to Adele when Ralph Tucker said nothing. She couldn't remember a time when he had managed to make a satisfactory response to some remark of his wife's. At the moment his head was lowered; his eyes were fixed on his bowl of cornflakes.

'You *do* have my trail mix, don't you, Ralph?' Noreen Tucker asked. 'We've got the trip to Abinger Manor this morning, and from what I could tell from looking at that brochure, it's going to be lots of walking. I'll need my nuts and chews. You haven't forgotten?'

Ralph shook his head.

'Because you did forget last week, sweetie, and the bus driver wasn't very pleased with us, was he, when we had to stop to get me a bite to eat at three o'clock?'

Ralph shook his head.

'So you *will* remember this time?'

'It's up in the room, hon. But I won't forget it.'

'That's good. Because . . .'

It was hard to believe that Noreen actually intended to go on, harder to believe that she could not see how tiresome she was. But she nattered happily for several more minutes until the arrival of Dolly Ragusa created a diversion.

Silently, Adele blessed the girl for having mercy upon them. She wouldn't have blamed Dolly for taking a place at another table. More than anyone, Dolly had a right to avoid the Tuckers, for she lived across the hall from them on the first floor of M staircase, so there could be no doubt that Dolly was well versed in the vicissitudes of Noreen Tucker's health. The words *my poor blood* were still ringing in the air when Dolly joined them, a black fedora pulled over her long blonde hair. She wrinkled her nose, rolled her eyes, then grinned.

Adele smiled. It was impossible not to like Dolly. She was the youngest student in the Great Houses class – a twenty-three-year-old art history graduate from the University of Chicago – but she moved among the older students with an easy confidence that Adele admired and a spirit she envied.

Dolly reached for the pitcher of orange juice as Howard Breen said to Adele, 'The Cleareys had a real blow-out this morning. Six-thirty. I thought Frances was going to put Sam through the window. Did you hear them?'

The question was spoken in an undertone, but Noreen looked up from straightening the sailor collar on her dress. 'A fight?'

The two words were spoken casually enough, but Adele saw how the information had piqued Noreen's interest. She had made no secret of her fascination with Sam Clearey, a U.C. Berkeley botanist.

'I was talking to Adele,' Howard said, not unkindly. 'You might have misheard.'

'I don't think that's the case,' Noreen replied. 'Six-thirty in the morning? A fight? About what?'

'Maybe he was out after curfew,' Adele said to deflect her. She felt Howard's foot hit hers beneath the table. Her sardonic remark – it seemed – had struck the truth.

'What a delicious thought!' Noreen rejoined. 'Was he out on the town or in on the bed? And whose?' She laughed and cast her eyes round the table. They settled on Dolly speculatively.

'I love these Cambridge intrigues,' Dolly said, 'Just like high school all over again.'

'The walls are thin, Dolly dear,' Noreen pointed out.

Dolly laughed, unaffected. 'You have got to be kidding. He's sixty years old, Noreen. Come on.' She twirled a lock of hair around her finger and looked reflective. 'But he is pretty great for an older guy, isn't he? All that grey hair. And the way he dresses. I wonder who snagged him?'

'I saw him in the bar last night with that blonde

from the Austen class,' Howard Breen offered.

Noreen Tucker's lips pursed. 'I hardly think that Sam Clearey would be taken in by a forty-nine-year-old divorcée with three teenagers and dyed hair. He's a college professor, Howard. He has taste. And intelligence. And breeding.'

'Thanks. You *were* talking about me, I assume?' Cleve Houghton slid into place next to Dolly Ragusa, carrying a plate heaped with eggs and sausages, grilled tomatoes and mushrooms.

Adele felt a quick release of tension at Cleve's arrival. Through mentioning the fact that Sam Clearey had shown interest in another woman, Howard Breen had innocently raised Noreen's ire. And Noreen was not the type of woman to let such a slight go by unanswered. Cleve's presence prevented her from doing so for the moment.

'Ran eight miles this morning,' he was saying. 'Along the backs to Granchester. The rest of you should try it. Hell, it's the best exercise known to man.' He tossed back his hair and contemplated Adele with a lazy smile. 'The *second* best exercise, that is.'

Heat took Adele's face. She crumpled her napkin in her fist.

'Goodness. In mixed company, Cleve.' Noreen Tucker's gaze was hungrily taking in the most salient aspect of Cleve Houghton's figure: jeans sculpted to muscular thighs. He was fifty but looked at least a decade younger.

'Damn right in mixed company,' Cleve Houghton replied. 'Wouldn't consider it in any other kind.'

'I certainly hope not,' Noreen declared. 'There's nothing worse than a man wasting himself on another man, is there? In one of my novels, I deal with just that topic. A woman falls in love with a homo and saves him. And when he realizes what it's like to have a woman and be normal, he melts. Just melts. I called it *Wild Seed of Passion*. *Seed* seemed appropriate. There's something in the Bible about spilling seed, isn't there? And that's exactly what those homos are up to. If you ask me, all they need is a real womanly woman and that would take care of that. Don't you agree, Howard?'

'I'd no idea you'd done research in this area,' he said.

'I . . . research?' Noreen pressed a hand to her chest. 'Don't be silly. It's only reasonable to assume that when a man and a woman . . . Heavens, surely I don't have to point out the obvious to *you*? Besides, a creative artist sometimes has to take licence with—'

'Reality? The truth? What?' Howard spoke pleasantly enough, but Adele saw the tightening muscles of his hand and she knew very well that Noreen saw the same.

Noreen reached across the table and patted his arm. 'Now confess to us, Howard. Are you one of those San Francisco liberals with half a dozen homosexual friends? Have I offended you? I'm just an old-fashioned girl who loves romance. And romance is all about true love, which as we all know can only exist between a man and a woman. You know that, don't you?' She smiled at him coolly. 'If you don't, you can ask our little Dolly. Or Cleve here. Or even Adele.'

Howard Breen stood. 'I'll forgo that pleasure for now,' he said, and left them.

'Whoa. What's the matter with him?' Dolly Ragusa asked, her fork poised in midair.

Cleve Houghton lifted a hand, dropped it to dangle limply from his wrist. 'Howard's a hell of a lot more likely to chase after me than you.' he said.

'Oh, Cleve!' Noreen Tucker chuckled, but Adele did not miss the glint of malicious triumph in her eyes. She excused herself and went in search of Howard.

She didn't find him until 8:45, when she went to join the rest of the Great Houses class at their appointed meeting place: the Queen's Gate of St Stephen's College. He was leaning against the arch of the gateway, stuffing a lunch bag into his tattered rucksack.

'You all right?' Adele took her own lunch from the box in which the kitchen staff had deposited it.

'I took a walk along the river to cool off.'

Howard didn't look that composed, no matter his words. A tautness in his features hadn't been there earlier. Even though she knew it was a lie, Adele said, 'I don't think she really knew what she was saying. Obviously, she *doesn't* know about you or she wouldn't have brought the subject up at all.'

He gave a sharp, unamused laugh. 'Don't kid yourself. She's a viper. She knows what she's doing.'

'Hey, you two. Smile!' Some ten yards away, Dolly Ragusa held a camera poised. She was making adjustments to an enormous telephoto lens.

'What are you shooting with that thing, our nostrils?' Howard asked.

Dolly laughed. 'It's a macro-zoom. Wide angles. Close-ups. It does everything but wash the dishes.'

Nearby, Cleve Houghton was pulling on a sweater. 'Why are you carting that thing around anyway? It looks like a pain.'

Dolly snapped his picture before she answered. 'Art historians always have cameras smashed up to their faces. Like extra appendages. That's how you recognize us.'

'I thought that's how you recognize Japanese tourists.' Sam Clearey spoke as he rounded the yew hedge that separated the main court from the interior of the college. As had been his habit for all their excursions, he was nattily dressed in tweeds, and his grey hair gleamed. His wife, a few steps behind him, however, looked terrible. Her eyes were bloodshot and her nose was puffy.

Seeing Frances Clearey, Adele felt a perfect crescent of pain in her chest. It came from recognizing a fellow sufferer. *Men are such shits*, she thought, and was about to join Frances and offer her the distraction of conversation when Victoria Wilder-Scott steamed down from Q staircase and rushed to join them, clipboard in hand.

'Right,' she said, breezily. 'You've read your brochures, I trust? And the section in *Great Houses of the Isles*? So you know we've dozens of things to see at Abinger Manor. That marvellous collection of rococo silver you saw in your text-book. The paintings by Gainsborough, Le Brun, Lorrain, Reynolds. That lovely piece by Whistler. The Holbein. Some remarkable furniture. The gardens are exquisite, and the park . . . You have your notebooks? Your cameras?'

'Dolly seems to be taking pictures for all of us,' Howard Breen said as Dolly snapped one of their instructor.

Victoria Wilder-Scott blinked at the girl, then

beamed. She made no secret of the fact that Dolly was her favourite student. They shared a similar education in art history and a mutual passion for *objets d'art*.

'Right. Then, shall we be off?' Victoria said. 'We're all here? No. Where are the Tuckers?'

The Tuckers arrived as she asked the question, Ralph shoving a plastic bag of trail mix into the front of his safari jacket while Noreen stooped to pick up their lunches, opened hers, and grimaced at its contents.

Her students assembled, Victoria Wilder-Scott lifted an umbrella to point the way and led them out of the college, over the bridge, and down Garret Hostel Lane toward the minibus.

Adele thought that Noreen Tucker intended to use their walk to the minibus as an opportunity to mend her fences with Howard, for the romance writer joined them with an alacrity that suggested some positive underlying intent. In a moment, however, her purpose became clear as she gave her attention to Sam Clearey, who apparently had decided that a walk with Howard and Adele was preferable to his wife's hostile silence. Noreen slipped her hand into the crook of his arm. She smiled at Howard and Adele, an invitation to become her fellow conspirators in whatever was to follow.

Adele shrank from the idea, feeling torn between walking more quickly in an attempt to leave Noreen behind and remaining where she was in the hope that somehow she might protect Sam, as she had been unable to protect Howard earlier. The nobler motive was ascendant. She remained with the little group, hating herself for being such a sop but unable to abandon Sam to Noreen, no matter how much he might deserve five minutes of her barbed conversation. She was, Adele noted, even now winding up the watch of her wit.

'I understand you were a naughty little boy last night,' Noreen said. 'The walls have ears, you know.'

Sam seemed to be in no mood to be teased. 'They don't need to have ears. Frances makes sure of that.'

'Are we to know the lady who was favoured with your charms? No, don't tell us. Let me guess.' Noreen played her fingers along the length of her hair. It was cut in a shoulder-length pageboy with a fringe of bangs, its colour several shades too dark for her skin.

'Have you read the brochure on Abinger Manor?' Adele asked.

The attempt to thwart Noreen was a poor one, and she countered without a glance in Adele's direction. 'I doubt our Sam's had much time to read. Affairs of the heart always take precedence, don't they?' She gave a soft, studied laugh. 'Just ask our Dolly.'

Ahead of them, Dolly's laughter rang out. She was walking with Cleve Houghton, gesturing to the spires of Trinity College to their right and bobbing her head emphatically to underscore a comment she was making.

With Sam within her grasp, Noreen's suddenly dropping the subject of his assignation on the previous night and moving on to target Dolly seemed out of character. It was not quite in keeping with Noreen's penchant for public humiliation, especially since there was no chance that Dolly could hear her words.

'Just look at them,' Noreen said, 'Dolly's digging for gold and she's found the mother lode, apparently.'

'Cleve Houghton?' Howard said. 'He's probably older than her father.'

'What does age matter? He's a doctor. Divorced. Piles of money. I've heard Dolly sighing over those slides Victoria shows us. You know the ones. Antiques, jewellery, paintings. Cleve's just the one to give her that sort of thing. And he'd be happy to do so, make no mistake of that.'

Sam Clearey said, 'She doesn't seem the type—'

Noreen squeezed his arm. 'What a gentleman you are, Sam. But you didn't see them in the bar last night. With Cleve holding forth about seducing women by getting to know their souls and appealing to their minds, and all the time his eyes were just boring into Dolly. Ask Adele. She was sitting right next to him, weren't you, dear? Lapping up every word like a thirsty cat.'

Noreen's teeth glittered in a feral smile, and for the first time Adele felt the bite of the woman's words directed against herself. A chill swept over her at the realization that nothing escaped Noreen's observation. For she *had* listened to Cleve. She had heard it all.

'Little Dolly may like to play virgin in the bush,' Noreen concluded placidly, 'but if Cleve Houghton's doing eight miles in the morning, I'd bet they're right between Dolly's legs. She's across the hall from me, Sam. And as I told you, the walls have ears.'

Sam disengaged Noreen's hand from his arm. 'Yes. Well. If you'll excuse me, I'd better see to Frances.'

Once he had gone, Noreen Tucker seemed to feel little need to remain with Howard and Adele. She left them to themselves and went to join her husband.

'Still think she doesn't mean any harm?' Howard asked. When Adele didn't reply, he looked her way.

She tried to smile, tried to shrug, failed at both, and hated herself for losing her composure in front of him. As she knew he would, Howard saw past the surface.

'She got to you,' he said.

Adele looked from Dolly Ragusa to Cleve Houghton

to Sam Clearey. She had received Noreen's message without any difficulty. Nasty though it was, it was loud. It was clear. As had been her message to Howard at breakfast. As, no doubt, had been her message to Sam Clearey.

'She's a viper,' Adele agreed.

The worst part of those brief moments with Noreen was the fact that her cruelty brought everything back in a rush. No matter that there was no direct correlation between Noreen's comment and the past; her veiled declaration of knowledge did more than merely make perilous inroads into Adele's need for privacy. It forced her to remember.

The minibus trundled along the narrow road. Signposts flashed by intermittently: Little Abington, Linton, Horseheath, Haverhill. Around Adele, the noise of conversation broke into Victoria Wilder-Scott's amplified monologue, which was droning endlessly from the front of the bus. Adele stared out the window.

She had been thirty-one and three years divorced when she'd met Bob. He'd been thirty-eight and eleven years married. He had three children and a wife who sewed and swept and ironed and packed lunches. She was loyal, devoted, and supportive. But she didn't have passion, Bob declared. She didn't speak to his soul. Only Adele spoke to his soul.

Adele believed it. Belief gave dignity to what otherwise would have been just a squalid affair. Elevated to a spiritual plane, their relationship was justified. More, it was sanctified. Having found her soul mate, she grew adept at rationalizing why she couldn't live without him. And how quickly five years had passed in this manner. How easily they decimated her meagre self-esteem.

It was two months now since Bob had been gone from her life. She felt like an open wound. 'You'll be back,' he'd said. 'You'll never have with another man what you have with me.' It was true. Circumstances had proven him correct.

'You can't get anything inside the bus. There's not enough light.'

Adele roused herself to see that Cleve Houghton was chuckling at Dolly Ragusa. She was kneeling on the seat in front of him, focusing her camera on his swarthy face.

'Sure I can.' *Click.*

'Then let me take one of you.'

'No way.'

'Come on.' He reached out.

She dodged him by slipping into the aisle. She moved among the seats, photographing one student after another: Ralph Tucker dozing with his head against the window, Howard Breen reading the brochure on Abinger Manor, Sam Clearey turning from the scenery outside as she called his name.

From the front of the minibus, Victoria Wilder-Scott continued her monologue about the Manor. '. . . family remained staunchly Royalist to the end. In the north tower, you'll see a priest's hole where Charles II was hidden prior to escaping to the Continent. And in the long gallery, you'll be challenged to find a Gibb door that's completely concealed. It was through this door that King Charles—'

'Doesn't she think we can read the brochure? We know all about the paintings and the furniture and the silver gee-gaws, for God's sake.' Noreen Tucker examined her teeth in the mirror of a compact. She rubbed at a spot of lipstick and got to her feet – intent, it seemed, upon Sam Clearey, who sat apart from his wife.

Restlessly, Adele turned in her seat. Her eyes met Cleve Houghton's. His gaze was frank and direct, the sort of appraisal that peeled off clothing and judged the flesh beneath.

He smiled. 'Things on your mind?' he asked.

Dolly provided Adele with an excuse not to answer. She was perched on the arm of Ralph Tucker's seat, talking cheerfully to Frances Clearey.

'I think it's great that you and Sam do things like this together,' Dolly said. 'This Cambridge course. I tried to get my boyfriend to come with me, but he wouldn't even consider it.'

Frances Clearey made an effort to smile, but it was evident that her concentration was on Noreen Tucker, who had dropped into the vacant seat next to Frances's husband.

'D'you two do this sort of thing every summer?' Dolly asked.

'This is our first time.' Frances's eyes flicked to

the side as Noreen Tucker laughed and inclined her head in Sam Clearey's direction.

Adele saw Dolly move so that her body blocked Frances's view of Sam and Noreen. 'I'm going to tell David – that's my boyfriend – all about you two. If a marriage is going to work, it seems to me that the husband and wife need to share mutual interests. And still give each other space at the same time. Like you and Sam. David and I . . . he can really be possessive.'

'I'm surprised he didn't come with you, then.'

'Oh, this is educational. David doesn't worry if I'm involved in art history. It's like him and his monkeys. He's a physical anthropologist. Howlers.'

'Howlers?'

Dolly lifted her camera and snapped Frances's picture. 'Howler monkeys. That's what he studies. Their poop, if you can believe it. I ask him what he's going to learn from putting monkey poop under a microscope. He says looking at it's not so bad. Collecting it is hell.'

Frances Clearey smiled. Dolly laughed.

Adele marvelled at how easily the girl had managed to bring Frances out of herself, even for a moment. How wise she was to point out subtly to Frances the strengths of her marriage instead of allowing her to sit in solitude, brooding upon its most evident weakness. Noreen Tucker was nothing, Dolly was saying. Other women are nothing. Sam belongs to you.

Dolly's was a decidedly insouciant attitude toward life. But why should she offer any other perspective? Her future stretched before her, uncomplicated and carefree. She had no past to haunt her. She was, at the heart of it, so wonderfully young.

'Why so solemn this morning?' Cleve Houghton asked Adele from across the aisle. 'Don't take yourself so seriously. Start enjoying yourself. Life's to be lived.'

Adele's throat tightened. She'd had quite enough of living.

Click.

'Adele!' Dolly was back with her camera.

When they arrived at their destination, the sight of

Abinger Manor roused Adele from her blackness of mood. Across a moat that was studded with lily pads, two crenellated towers stood at the sides of the building's front entry. On either side of them, crow-stepped gables were surmounted by impossibly tall, impossibly decorated chimneys. Bay windows, a later addition to the house, extended over the moat and gave visual access to an extensive garden. This was edged on one side with a tall yew hedge and on the other with a brick wall against which grew an herbaceous border of lavender, aster, and dianthus. The Great Houses of Britain class wandered toward this garden with a quarter of an hour to explore it prior to the Manor's first tour.

Adele saw that they were not to be the only visitors to the Manor that morning. A large group of Germans debouched from a tour coach and joined Dolly Ragusa in extensively photographing the garden and the exterior of the house. Two family groups entered the maze and began shouting at one another as they immediately lost their way. A handsome couple pulled into the car park in a silver Bentley and stood in conversation next to the moat. For a moment, Adele thought that these last visitors were actually the owners of the Manor – they were extremely well dressed and the Bentley suggested a wealth unassociated with taking tours of great houses. But they joined the others in the garden, and as they strolled past Adele, she overheard a snatch of conversation pass between them.

'Really, Tommy, darling, I can't recall agreeing to come here at all. Is this one of your tricks?'

'Salmon sandwiches,' was the man's unaccountable reply.

'Salmon sandwiches?'

'I bribed you, Helen. Early last week. A picnic. Salmon sandwiches. Stilton cheese. Strawberry tarts. White wine.'

'Ah. *Those* salmon sandwiches.'

They laughed together quietly. The man dropped his arm around the woman's shoulders. He was tall, very blond, clear-featured, and handsome. She was slender, dark-haired, with an oval face. They walked in perfect rhythm with each other. Lovers, Adele thought bleakly, and forced herself to turn away.

When a bell rang to call them for the tour,

Adele went gratefully, hoping for distraction, never realizing how thorough that distraction would be.

Their guide was a determined-looking girl in her mid-twenties with pimples on her chin and too much eye make-up. She spoke in staccato. They were in the original screens passage, she told them. The wall to their left was the original screen. They would be able to admire its carving when they got to the other side of it. If they would please stay together and not stray behind the corded-off areas . . . Photographs were permissible without a flash.

As the group moved forward, Adele found herself wedged between two German matrons who needed to bathe. She breathed shallowly and was thankful when the size of the Great Hall allowed the crowd to spread out.

It was a magnificent room, everything that Victoria Wilder-Scott, their textbook, and the Abinger Manor brochure had promised it would be. While the guide catalogued its features for them, Adele dutifully took note of the towering coved ceiling, of the minstrel gallery and its intricate fretwork, of the tapestries, the portraits, the fireplace, the marble floor. Near her, cameras focused and shutters clicked. And then at her ear: 'Just what I was looking for. *Just.*'

Adele's heart sank. She had successfully avoided Noreen Tucker in the garden, after having almost stumbled upon her and Ralph in the middle of a Noreenian rhapsody over a stone bench upon which she had determined the lovers in her new romance novel would have their climactic assignation.

'The ball. Right in here!' Noreen went on. 'Oh, I *knew* we were clever to take this class, Ralph!'

Adele looked Noreen's way. She was dipping her hand into the plastic bag that protruded from her husband's safari jacket. Ten o'clock, Adele thought, trail-mix time. Noreen munched away, murmuring, 'Charles and Delfinia clasped each other as the music from the gallery floated to caress them. "This is madness, darling. We must not. We cannot." He refused to listen. "We *must*. Tonight." So they—'

Adele walked away, grateful for the moment when the guide began ushering them out of the Great Hall.

They went up a flight of stairs and into a narrow, lengthy gallery.

'This long gallery is one of the most famous in England,' their guide informed them as they assembled behind a cord that ran the length of the room. 'It contains not only one of the finest collections of rococo silver, which you see arranged to the left of the fireplace on a demilune table – that's a Sheraton piece, by the way – but also a Le Brun, two Gainsboroughs, a Reynolds, a Holbein, a charming Whistler, and several lesser-known artists. In the case at the end of the room you'll find a hat, gloves, and stockings that belonged to Queen Elizabeth I. And here's one of the most remarkable features of the room.'

She walked to the left of the Sheraton table and pushed lightly on a section of the panelling. A door swung open, previously hidden by the structure of the wall.

'It's a Gibb door. Clever, isn't it? Servants could come and go through it and never be seen in the public rooms of the house.'

Cameras clicked. Necks craned. Voices murmured.

'And if you'll especially take note of—'

'Ralph!' Noreen Tucker gasped. '*Ralph!*'

Adele was among those who turned at the interruption. Noreen was standing just outside the cord, next to a satinwood table on which sat a china bowl of potpourri. She was quite pale, her eyes wide, her extended hand trembling. Hypoglycaemia seemed to be getting the better of her.

'Nor? *Hon?* Oh, damn, her blood—' Ralph Tucker had no chance to finish. With an inarticulate cry, Noreen fell across the table, splintering the bowl and scattering potpourri across the Persian carpet. Down the length of the room, the satin cord ripped from the posts that held it in place as Noreen Tucker crashed through it on her way to the floor.

Adele found herself immobilized, although around her, everyone else seemed to move at once. She felt caught up in a swell as some people pressed forward toward the fallen woman and others backed away. Someone screamed. Someone else called upon the Lord. Three Germans dropped in shock onto the couches that were made available to them now that the cord of demarcation was gone. There was a cry for water, a shout for air.

Ralph Tucker shrieked, 'Noreen!' and dropped to his knees amid the potpourri and china. He pulled at his wife's shoulder. She had fallen on her face, her straw hat rolling across the carpet.

Adele called wildly, 'Cleve. *Cleve*,' and then he was pushing through the crowd. He turned Noreen over, took one look at her face, and began administering CPR. 'Get an ambulance!' he ordered.

Adele swung around to do so. Their tour guide was rooted to her spot next to the fireplace, her attention fixed upon the woman on the floor as if she herself had had a part in putting her there.

'An ambulance!' Adele cried.

Voices came from everywhere.

'Is she . . .'

'God, she *can't* be . . .'

'Noreen! Nor! Hon!'

'Sie ist gerade ohnmächtig geworden, nicht wahr . . .'

'Get an ambulance, goddamn it!' Cleve Houghton raised his head. 'Move!' he yelled at the guide.

She flew through the Gibb door and pounded up the stairs.

Cleve paused, took Noreen's pulse. He forced her mouth open and attempted to resuscitate her.

'Noreen!' Ralph wailed.

'Kann er nicht etwas unternehmen?'

'Doesn't anyone . . .'

'Schauen Sie sich die Gesichtsfarbe an.'

'She's gone.'

'It's no use.'

'Diese dummen Amerikaner!'

Over the swarm, Adele saw the blond man from the Bentley remove his jacket and hand it to his companion. He eased through the crowd, straddled Noreen, and took over CPR as Cleve Houghton continued his efforts to get her to breathe.

'Noreen! Hon!'

'Get him out of the way!'

Adele took Ralph's arm, attempting to ease him to his feet. 'Ralph, if you'll let them—'

'She needed to eat!'

Victoria Wilder-Scott joined them. 'Please, Mr Tucker. If you'll give them a chance . . .'

The tour guide crashed back into the room.

'I've phoned . . .' She faltered, then stopped altogether.

Adele looked from the guide to Cleve. He had raised his head. His expression said it all.

Events converged. People reacted. Curiosity, sympathy, panic, aversion. Leadership was called for, and the blond man assumed it, wresting it from the guide with the simple words, 'I'm Thomas Lynley. Scotland Yard CID.' He showed her a piece of identification she seemed only too happy to acknowledge.

Thomas Lynley organized them quickly, in a manner that encouraged neither protest nor question. They would continue with the tour, he informed them, in order to clear the room for the arrival of the ambulance.

He remained behind with his companion, Ralph Tucker, Cleve Houghton, and the dead woman. Adele saw him bend, saw him open Noreen's clenched hand. Cleve said, 'Heart failure. I've seen them go like this before,' but although Lynley nodded, he looked not at Cleve but raised his head from examining Noreen's hand and focused on the group, his brown eyes speculating upon each one of them as they left the room. Ralph Tucker sank onto a delicate chair. Thomas Lynley's companion went to him, murmured a few words, put her hand on his shoulder.

Then the door closed behind them and the group was in the drawing room, being asked to examine the pendant plasterwork of its remarkable ceiling. It was called the King Edward Drawing Room, their much-subdued guide told them, its name taken from the statue of Edward IV that stood over the mantelpiece. It was a three-quarter-size statue, she explained, not life-size, for unlike most men of his time, Edward IV was well over six feet tall. In fact, when he rode into London on 26 February 1460 . . .

Adele did not see how the young woman could go on. There was something indecent about being asked to admire chandeliers, flocked wallpaper, eighteenth-century furniture, Chinese vases, and a French chimneypiece in the face of Noreen Tucker's death. Adele had certainly disliked Noreen, but death was death and it seemed that, out of respect to her passing, they might well have abandoned the rest of the tour and returned to Cambridge. She couldn't understand why Thomas Lynley had not instructed them to do so. Surely it would have been far more humane than to expect them to traipse round the rest of the house as if nothing had happened.

But even Ralph had wanted them to continue. 'You go on', he had said to Victoria when she had attempted to remain with him in the long gallery. 'People are depending on you.' He made it sound as if a tour of Abinger Manor were akin to a battle upon whose outcome the fate of a nation depended. It was just the sort of comment that would appeal to Victoria. So the tour continued.

Everyone was restless. The air was close. Composure seemed brittle. Adele had no doubt that she was not the only person longing to escape from Abinger Manor.

There was a murmur when Cleve Houghton rejoined them in the winter dining room.

'They've taken her,' he said in a low voice to Adele.

'And that man? The policeman?'

'Still in the gallery when I left. He's put out a call for the local police.'

'Why?' Adele asked. 'I saw him looking at . . . Cleve, you don't . . . She seemed healthy, didn't she?'

Cleve's eyes narrowed. 'I know a heart attack when I see one. Jesus, what are you thinking?'

Adele didn't know what she was thinking. She only knew that she had recognized something on Lynley's face when he had looked up from examining Noreen Tucker's trail mix. Consternation, suspicion, anger, outrage. Something had been there. If that were the case, then it could only mean one thing. Adele felt her stomach churn. She began to evaluate her fellow students in an entirely new way: as potential killers.

Frances Clearey seemed to have been shaken from her morning's fury at her husband. She was close at Sam's side, pressed to his arm. Perhaps Noreen's death had allowed her to see how fleeting life was, how insignificant its quarrels and concerns were once one came to terms with its finitude. Or perhaps she simply had nothing further to worry about now that Noreen was eliminated.

She hadn't been at breakfast, Adele recalled, so she could have slipped into Noreen's room and put something into her trail mix. Especially if she knew that Sam had spent the night with Noreen in town somewhere. Removing a rival to a man's love seemed an adequate motive for murder.

But Sam himself had also not been at breakfast. So he, too, had access to Noreen's supply of food. If Noreen had known with whom he had spent the night – and perhaps that's what she had been hinting at this morning – perhaps Sam had seen the need to be rid of her. Especially if she had been the woman herself.

It was hard to believe. Yet at the same time, looking at Sam, Adele could see how Noreen's death had affected him. Beneath his tan, his face was worn, his mouth set. His eyes seemed cloudy. In each room, they alighted first upon Dolly, as if her beauty were an anodyne for him.

Dolly herself had come into breakfast late, so she also had access to Noreen's supply of nuts.

But Noreen had not given Dolly an overt reason to harm her, and surely Noreen's gossip about the girl – even if Dolly had heard it, which was doubtful – would only have amused her.

As it would have amused Cleve Houghton. And pleased him. And swelled his ego substantially. Indeed, Cleve had every reason to keep Noreen alive. She had been doing wonders to build repute of his sexual prowess. On the other hand, Cleve had come into breakfast late, so he, too, had access to the Tuckers' room.

Howard Breen seemed to be the only one who hadn't had time to get to Noreen's trail mix. Except, Adele remembered, he had left breakfast early and she hadn't been able to find him.

Everyone, then, had the opportunity to mix something in with the nuts, raisins, and dried fruit. But what had that something been? And how on earth had someone managed to get hold of it? Surely one didn't walk into a Cambridge chemist's shop and ask for a quick-acting poison. So whoever tampered with the mix had to have experience with poisons, had to know what to expect.

They were in the library when Thomas Lynley and his lady rejoined them. He ran his eyes over everyone in the room. His companion did the same. He said something to her quietly, and the two of them separated, taking positions in different parts of the crowd. Neither of them paid the slightest attention to anything other than to the people. But they gave their full attention to them.

From the library they went into the chapel, accompanied only by the sounds of their own footsteps, the echoing voice of the guide, the snapping of cameras. Lynley moved through the group, saying nothing to anyone save to his companion, with whom he spoke a few words at the door. Again they separated.

From the chapel they went into the armoury. From there into the billiard room. From there to the music room. From there down two flights of stairs and into the kitchen. The buttery beyond it had been turned into a gift shop. The Germans made for this. The Americans began to do likewise. That was when Lynley spoke.

'If I might see everyone, please,' he said as they

began to scatter. 'If you'll just stay here in the kitchen for a moment.'

Protests rose from the German group. The Americans said nothing.

'We've a problem to consider,' Lynley told them, 'regarding Noreen Tucker's death.'

'Problem?' Behind Adele, Cleve Houghton spoke. Others chimed in.

'What do you want with us anyway?'

'What's going on?'

'It was heart failure,' Cleve asserted. 'I've seen enough of that to tell you—'

'As have I,' a heavily accented voice said. The speaker was a member of the German party, and he looked none too pleased that their tour was once again being disrupted. 'I am a doctor. I, too, have seen heart failure. I know what I see.'

Lynley extended his hand. In his palm lay a half dozen seeds. 'It looked like heart failure. That's what an alkaloid does. It paralyses the heart in a matter of minutes. These are yew, by the way.'

'Yew?'

'What was yew—'

'But she wouldn't—'

Adele kept her eyes on Lynley's palm. Seeds. Plants. The connection was horrible. She avoided looking at the one person in the kitchen who would know beyond a doubt the potential for harm contained in a bit of yew.

'Surely those came from the potpourri,' Victoria Wilder-Scott said. 'It spilled all over the carpet when Mrs Tucker fell.'

Lynley shook his head. 'They were mixed in with the nuts in her hand. And the bag her husband carried was thick with them. She was murdered.'

The Germans protested heartily at this. The doctor led them. 'You have no business with us. This woman was a stranger. I insist that we be allowed to leave.'

'Of course,' Lynley answered. 'As soon as we solve the problem of the silver.'

'What on earth are you talking about?'

'It appears that one of you took the opportunity of the chaos in the long gallery to remove two pieces of rococo silver from the table by the fireplace. They're salt cellars. Very small. And definitely missing. This isn't my jurisdiction, of course, but until the local police arrive to start their inquiries into Mrs Tucker's death, I'd like to take care of this small detail of the silver myself.'

'What are you going to do?' Frances Clearey asked.

'Do you plan to keep us here until one of us admits to something?' the German doctor scoffed. 'You cannot search us without some authority.'

'That's correct,' Lynley said. 'I can't search you. Unless you agree to be searched.'

Feet shuffled. A throat cleared. Urgent conversation was conducted in German. Someone rustled papers in a notebook.

Cleve Houghton was the first to speak. He looked over the group. 'Hell, I have no objection.'

'But the women . . .' Victoria pointed out.

Lynley nodded to his companion, who was standing by a display of copper kettles at the edge of the group. 'This is Lady Helen Clyde,' he told them. 'She'll search the women.'

As one body, they turned to Lynley's companion. Resting upon them, her dark eyes were friendly.

Her expression was gentle. What an absurdity it would be to resist cooperating with such a lovely creature.

The search was carried out in two rooms: the women in the scullery and the men in a warming room across the hall. In the scullery, Lady Helen made a thorough job of it. She watched each woman undress, redress. She emptied pockets, handbags, canvas totes. She checked the lining of raincoats. She opened umbrellas. All the time she chatted in a manner designed to put them at ease. She asked the Americans about their class, about Cambridge, about great houses they had seen and where they were from. She confided in the Germans about spending two weeks in the Black Forest one summer and confessed to an embarrassed dislike of the out-of-doors. She never mentioned the word *murder*. Aside from the operation in which they were engaged, they might have been new acquaintances talking over tea. Yet Adele saw for herself that Lady Helen was quite efficient at her job, for all her friendliness and good breeding. If she didn't work for the police herself – and her relationship with Lynley certainly did not suggest that she was employed by Scotland Yard – she certainly had knowledge of their procedures.

Nonetheless, she found nothing. Nor, apparently, did Lynley. When the two groups were gathered once again in the kitchen, Adele saw him shake his head at Lady Helen. If the silver had been taken, it was not being carried by anyone. Even Victoria Wilder-Scott and the tour guide had been searched.

Lynley told them to wait in the tearoom. He turned back to the stairway at the far end of the kitchen.

'Where's he going now?' Frances Clearey asked.

'He'll have to look for the silver in the rest of the house,' Adele said.

'But that could take forever!' Dolly protested.

'It doesn't matter, does it? We're going to have to wait to talk to the local police anyway.'

'It was heart failure,' Cleve said. 'There's no silver missing. It's probably being cleaned somewhere.'

Adele fell to the back of the crowd as they walked across the pebbled courtyard. A sense of unease plucked at her mind. It had been with her much of the morning, hidden like a secondary message between the lines of Noreen Tucker's words, trying to fight its way to the surface of her consciousness in the minibus, lying just beyond the range of her vision ever since they had arrived at the Manor. Like the children's game of What's Wrong With This Picture, there was a distortion somewhere. She could feel it distinctly. She simply couldn't see it.

Her thoughts tumbled upon one another without connection or reason, like images produced by a kaleidoscope. There were yew hedges in the courtyard of St Stephen's College. Sam and Frances Clearey had had a fight. The walls have ears. The silver was available. It was pictured in their text. It was in the brochures. They'd seen both in advance. Dolly wanted Cleve. She loved antiques. Sam Clearey liked women, liked the blonde from the Dickens class, liked . . .

Once again Adele saw Lady Helen go through their belongings. She saw her empty, probe, touch, leave nothing unexamined. She saw her shake her head at Lynley. She saw Lynley frown.

The two groups entered the tearoom and segregated themselves from each other. The Americans took positions at a refectory table at the far end. The Germans lined up for coffee and cakes.

'Victoria, can we go back to Cambridge?' Frances asked. 'I mean, when this is over? We've another house to see today, but we can drop it, can't we?'

Victoria was hesitant. 'Ralph did specifically want us to—'

'Screw Ralph Tucker!' Sam said. 'Come on, Victoria, we've had it.'

'There's the minibus to consider, the driver's salary . . .'

'Couldn't we just chip in some money and tip him or something?' Dolly set her camera on the table in front of her.

And there it was in an instant. Right before her. Adele saw it at last. She knew what Noreen Tucker had been saying during their walk to the bus. She knew the source of her own disquiet on the journey to Abinger Manor. She acknowledged what she had seen without seeing from the moment they had arrived at the Manor. Thirty-six was the key, but it had been exceeded long ago. The knowledge brought to Adele an attendant rush of wrenching illness. Thomas Lynley had made an assumption from the facts at hand.

But Lynley was wrong.

She pushed herself to her feet and left the group. Someone called after her, but she continued on her way. She found Lynley in the drawing room, directing three workmen who were crawling across the floor.

How can I do this? she asked herself. And then, *Why? With the future a blank slate upon which nothing but hope and success were written. Why?*

Lynley looked up. Lady Helen Clyde did likewise. Adele did not even have to speak to them. They joined her at once and followed her to the tearoom.

'What's going on?' Cleve asked.

Adele didn't look at him. 'Dolly, give the inspector your camera.'

Dolly's blue eyes widened. 'I don't understand.'

'Give him the camera, Dolly. Let him look at the lens.'

'But you—'

Lynley lifted the camera from the girl's shoulder. Lined along its strap were containers for film. All of them were empty. Adele had seen that earlier, had seen it and had thought no more about it than she had thought about the fact that there had been no film in Dolly's shoulder bag. Nor had there been any in her pockets. She'd been shooting pictures all morning with no film in her camera at all, in order to conceal her real reason for carrying the camera with her to the Manor in the first place.

Lynley twisted off the macro-zoom lens. It was useless, hollowed. Two pieces of rococo silver tumbled out.

Howard dropped into the seat next to Adele. 'You okay?'

'Okay.' She didn't want to talk about it. She felt like a Judas. She wanted to go home. She tried to keep from thinking about Dolly being led off by the police.

'How did you figure Dolly?'

'She took too many pictures. She would have had

to change film, but she never did that. Because there was no film.'

'But Noreen. Why did Dolly . . .'

Adele's limbs felt numb. 'I don't think she cared one way or the other about Noreen. Probably intended the seeds to make Noreen good and sick, not kill her. She just needed a diversion to get to the silver.'

'But could she possibly have known what yew seeds do?'

'Sam. He probably didn't know what he was telling her or why she was asking. He probably didn't think of anything except what it felt like to be his age and to be in bed with someone like Dolly.' Even that was hard to bear. Knowing that Dolly's solicitous conversation with Frances Clearey about her marriage had been nothing more than part of the game. Just another diversion, just another lie.

'*Sam* and Dolly?' Howard looked across the aisle to where Cleve Houghton lounged in his seat, eyes half closed. 'I thought Cleve . . . when Noreen was telling us that Cleve was talking last night about seducing women . . .'

'She was talking to me. About me. Cleve wasn't with Dolly last night, Howard.' Adele looked out the window, said nothing more. After a moment, she felt Howard leave the seat and move away.

I will bury you, Bob, she had thought with Cleve Houghton. *I will end it between us this way.* So she had drunk in the college bar with him, she had walked on the backs and listened to him talk, she had pretended to find him intriguing and delightful, a man of passion, a soul mate, a replacement for Bob. And when he wanted her, she had obliged. Hurried grappling, urgent coupling, a body in her bed. To feel alive, to feel wanted, to feel a creature of worth. But not to bury Bob. It hadn't worked that way.

'Hey.' Adele pretended not to hear him, but Cleve crossed the aisle and dropped into the seat. He carried a flask in his hand. 'You look like you need a drink. Hell, I need one.' He drank, spoke again in a lower voice. 'Tonight?'

Adele raised her eyes to his face, trying and failing to force his features into the shape of another man's.

'Well?' he said.

Of course, she thought. Why not? What difference did it make when life was so fleeting and youth without meaning?

'Sure,' she said. 'Tonight.'

I, Richard

I, Richard

Malcolm Cousins groaned in spite of himself. Considering his circumstances, this was the last sound he wanted to make. A sigh of pleasure or a moan of satisfaction would have been more appropriate. But the truth was simple and he had to face it: No longer was he the performance artist he once had been in the sexual arena. Time was when he could bonk with the best of them. But that time had gone the way of his hair and at forty-nine years old, he considered himself lucky to be able to get the appliance up and running twice a week.

He rolled off Betsy Perryman and thudded onto his back. His lower vertebrae were throbbing like drummers in a marching band, and the always-dubious pleasure he'd just taken from Betsy's corpulent, perfume-drenched charms was quickly transformed to a faint memory. Jesus God, he thought with a gasp. Forget justification altogether. Was the end even *worth* the bloody means?

Luckily, Betsy took the groan and the gasp the way Betsy took most everything. She heaved herself onto her side, propped her head upon the palm of her hand and observed him with an expression that was meant to be coy. The last thing Betsy wanted him to know was how desperate she was for him to be her lifeboat out of her current marriage – number four this one was – and Malcolm was only too happy to accommodate her in the fantasy. Sometimes it got a bit complicated, remembering what he was supposed to know and what he was supposed to be ignorant of, but he always found that if Betsy's suspicions about his sincerity became aroused, there was a simple and expedient, albeit back-troubling, way to assuage her doubts about him.

She reached for the tangled sheet, pulled it up, and extended a plump hand. She caressed his hairless pate and smiled at him lazily. 'Never did it with a baldy before. Have I told you that, Malc?'

Every single time the two of them – as she so poetically stated – did it, he recalled. He thought of Cora, the springer spaniel bitch he'd adored in childhood, and the memory of the dog brought suitable fondness to his face. He eased Betsy's fingers down his cheek and kissed each one of them.

'Can't get enough, naughty boy,' she said. 'I've never had a man like you, Malc Cousins.'

She scooted over to his side of the bed, closer and closer until her huge bosoms were less than an inch from his face. At this proximity, her cleavage resembled Cheddar Gorge and was just about as appealing a sexual object. God, another go round? he thought. He'd be dead before he was fifty if they went on like this. And not a step nearer to his objective.

He nuzzled within the suffocating depths of her mammaries, making the kinds of yearning noises that she wanted to hear. He did a bit of sucking and then made much of catching sight of his wrist-watch on the bedside table.

'Christ!' He grabbed the watch for a feigned better look. 'Jesus, Betsy, it's eleven o'clock. I told those Aussie Ricardians I'd meet them at Bosworth Field at noon. I've got to get rolling.'

Which is what he did, right out of bed before she could protest. As he shrugged into his dressing gown, she struggled to transform his announcement into something comprehensible. Her face screwed up and she said, 'Those Ozzirecordians? What the hell's that?' She sat up, her blonde hair matted and snarled and most of her make-up smeared from her face.

'Not Ozzirecordians,' Malcolm said. 'Aussie. Australian. Australian Ricardians. I told you about them last week, Betsy.'

'Oh, that.' She pouted. 'I thought we could have a picnic lunch today.'

'In this weather?' He headed for the bathroom. It wouldn't do to arrive for the tour reeking of sex and Shalimar. 'Where did you fancy having a picnic in January? Can't you hear that wind? It must be ten below outside.'

'A bed picnic,' she said. 'With honey and cream.

You *said* that was your fantasy. Or don't you remember?'

He paused in the bedroom doorway. He didn't much like the tone of her question. It made a demand that reminded him of everything he hated about women. Of *course* he didn't remember what he'd claimed to be his fantasy about honey and cream. He'd said lots of things over the past two years of their liaison. But he'd forgotten most of them once it had become apparent that she was seeing him as he wished to be seen. Still, the only course was to play along. 'Honey and cream,' he sighed. 'You brought honey and cream? Oh Christ, Bets . . .' A quick dash back to the bed. A tonguely examination of her dental work. A frantic clutching between her legs. 'God, you're going to drive me mad, woman. I'll be walking round Bosworth with my prong like a poker all day.'

'Serves you right,' she said pertly and reached for his groin. He caught her hand in his.

'You love it,' he said.

'No more'n you.'

He sucked her fingers again. 'Later,' he said. 'I'll

trot those wretched Aussies round the battlefield and if you're still here then ... You know what happens next.'

'It'll be too late then. Bernie thinks I've only gone to the butcher.'

Malcolm favoured her with a pained look, the better to show that the thought of her hapless and ignorant husband – his old best friend Bernie – scored his soul. 'Then there'll be another time. There'll be hundreds of times. With honey and cream. With caviar. With oysters. Did I ever tell you what I'll do with the oysters?'

'What?' she asked.

He smiled. 'Just you wait.'

He retreated to the bathroom, where he turned on the shower. As usual, an inadequate spray of lukewarm water fizzled out of the pipe. Malcolm shed his dressing gown, shivered, and cursed his circumstances. Twenty-five years in the classroom, teaching history to spotty-faced hooligans who had no interest in anything beyond the immediate gratification of their sweaty-palmed needs, and what did he have to show for it? Two up and two down in an ancient terraced house down the street from Gloucester Grammar. An ageing Vauxhall with no spare tyre. A mistress with an agenda for marriage and a taste for kinky sex. And a passion for a long dead King that – he was determined – would be the wellspring from which would flow his future. The means were so close, just tantalizing centimetres from his eager grasp. And once his reputation was secured, the book contracts, the speaking engagements, and the offers of gainful employment would follow.

'Shit!' he bellowed as the shower water went from warm to scalding without a warning. 'Damn!' He fumbled for the taps.

'Serves you right,' Betsy said from the doorway. 'You're a naughty boy and naughty boys need punishing.'

He blinked water from his eyes and squinted at her. She'd put on his best flannel shirt – the very one he'd intended to wear on the tour of Bosworth Field, blast the woman – and she lounged against the doorjamb in her best attempt at a seductive pose. He ignored her and went about his showering. He could tell she was determined to have her way, and her way was another bonk before he left. Forget it, Bets, he said to her silently. Don't push your luck.

'I don't understand you, Malc Cousins,' she said. 'You're the only man in civilization who'd rather tramp round a soggy pasture with a bunch of tourists than cozy up in bed with the woman he says he loves.'

'Not says, does,' Malcolm said automatically. There was a dreary sameness to their post-coital conversations that was beginning to get him decidedly down.

'That so? I wouldn't've known. I'd've said you fancy whatsisname the King a far sight more'n you fancy me.'

Well, Richard was definitely more interesting a character, Malcolm thought. But he said, 'Don't be daft. It's money for our nest egg anyway.'

'We don't need a nest egg,' she said. 'I've told you that about a hundred times. We've got the—'

'Besides,' he cut in hastily. There couldn't be too little said between them on the subject of Betsy's expectations. 'It's good experience. Once the book

is finished, there'll be interviews, personal appear-
ances, lectures. I need the practice. I need' – this
with a winning smile in her direction – 'more than
an audience of one, my darling. Just think what
it'll be like, Bets. Cambridge, Oxford, Harvard, the
Sorbonne. Will you like Massachusetts? What about
France?'

'Bernie's heart's giving him trouble again, Malc,'
Betsy said, running her finger up the doorjamb.

'Is it, now?' Malcolm said happily. 'Poor old
Bernie. Poor bloke, Bets.'

The problem of Bernie had to be handled, of course.
But Malcolm was confident that Betsy Perryman
was up for the challenge. In the afterglow of sex
and inexpensive champagne, she'd told him once
that each one of her four marriages had been a
step forward and upward from the marriage that
had preceded it, and it didn't take a hell of a lot
of brains to know that moving out of a marriage
to a dedicated inebriate – no matter how affable –
into a relationship with a school teacher on his way
to unveiling a piece of mediaeval history that would

set the country on its ear was a step in the right direction. So Betsy would definitely handle Bernie. It was only a matter of time.

Divorce was out of the question, of course. Malcolm had made certain that Betsy understood that while he was desperate mad hungry and all the etceteras for a life with her, he would no more ask her to come to him in his current impoverished circumstances than would he expect the next Princess of Wales to take up life in a bed-sit on the south bank of the Thames. Not only would he not ask that of her, he wouldn't allow it. Betsy – his beloved – deserved so much more than he would be able to give her, such as he was. But when his ship came in, darling Bets . . . Or if, God forbid, anything should ever happen to Bernie . . . This, he hoped, was enough to light a fire inside the spongy grey mass that went for her brain.

Malcolm felt no guilt at the thought of Bernie Perryman's demise. True, they'd known each other in childhood as sons of mothers who'd been girl-hood friends. But they'd parted ways at the end of adolescence, when poor Bernie's failure to pass more than one A-level had doomed him to life on the family farm while Malcolm had gone on to University. And after that . . . well, differing levels of education *did* take a toll on one's ability to communicate with one's erstwhile – and less educated – mates, didn't it? Besides, when Malcolm returned from University, he could see that his old friend had sold his soul to the Black Bush devil, and what would it profit him to renew a friendship with the district's most prominent drunk? Still, Malcolm liked to think he'd taken a modicum of pity on Bernie Perryman. Once a month for years, he'd gone to the farmhouse – under cover of darkness, of course – to play chess with his former friend and to listen to his inebriated musings about their childhood and the what-might-have-beens.

Which was how he first found out about The Legacy, as Bernie had called it. Which was what he'd spent the last two years bonking Bernie's wife in order to get his hands on. Betsy and Bernie had no children. Bernie was the last of his line. The Legacy was going to come to Betsy. And Betsy was going to give it to Malcolm.

She didn't know that yet. But she would soon enough.

Malcolm smiled, thinking of what Bernie's legacy would do to further his career. For nearly ten years, he'd been writing furiously on what he'd nicknamed *Dickon Delivered* – his untarnishing of the reputation of Richard III – and once The Legacy was in his hands, his future was going to be assured. As he rolled towards Bosworth Field and the Australian Ricardians awaiting him there, he recited the first line of the penultimate chapter of his magnum opus. 'It is with the alleged disappearance of Edward the Lord Bastard, Earl of Pembroke and March, and Richard, Duke of York, that historians have traditionally begun to rely upon sources contaminated by their own self-interest.'

God, it was beautiful writing, he thought. And better than that, it was the truth as well.

The tour coach was already there when Malcolm roared into the car park at Bosworth Field. Its occupants had foolishly disembarked. All apparently female and of depressingly advanced years, they were huddled into a shivering pack, looking sheep-like and abandoned in the gale-force winds that were blowing. When Malcolm heaved himself out of his car, one of their number disengaged herself from their midst and strode towards him. She was sturdily built and much younger than the rest, which gave Malcolm hope of being able to grease his way through the moment with some generous dollops of charm. But then he noted her short clipped hair, elephantine ankles, and massive calves . . . not to mention the clipboard that she was smacking into her hand as she walked. An unhappy lesbian tour guide out for blood, he thought. God, what a deadly combination.

Nonetheless, he beamed a glittering smile in her direction. 'Sorry,' he sang out. 'Blasted car trouble.'

'See here, mate,' she said in the unmistakable discordant twang – all long a's becoming long i's – of a denizen of Deepest Down Under, 'when Romance of Great Britain pays for a tour at noon, Romance of Great Britain expects the bleeding tour to begin at noon. So why're you late? Christ, it's like Siberia out here. We could die of exposure. Jaysus, let's just get on with it.' She turned on her heel and waved her charges over towards the edge of the car park where the footpath carved a trail round the circumference of the battlefield.

Malcolm dashed to catch up. His tips hanging in the balance, he would have to make up for his tardiness with a dazzling show of expertise.

'Yes, yes,' he said with insincere joviality as he reached her side. 'It's incredible that you should mention Siberia, Miss . . . ?'

'Sludgecur,' she said, and her expression dared him to react to the name.

'Ah. Yes. Miss Sludgecur. Of course. As I was saying, it's incredible that you should mention Siberia because this bit of England has the highest elevation west of the Urals. Which is why we have these rather Muscovian temperatures. You can imagine what it might have been like in the fifteenth century when—'

'We're not here for meteorology,' she barked. 'Get on with it before my ladies freeze their arses off.'

Her ladies tittered and clung to one another in

the wind. They had the dried apple faces of octogenarians, and they watched Sludgecur with the devotion of children who'd seen their parent take on all comers and deck them unceremoniously.

'Yes, well,' Malcolm said. 'The weather's the principal reason that the battlefield's closed in the winter. We made an exception for your group because they're fellow Ricardians. And when fellow Ricardians come calling at Bosworth, we like to accommodate them. It's the best way to see that the truth gets carried forward, as I'm sure you'll agree.'

'What the bloody hell are you yammering about?' Sludgecur asked. 'Fellow who? Fellow what?'

Which should have told Malcolm that the tour wasn't going to proceed as smoothly as he had hoped. 'Ricardians,' he said and beamed at the elderly women surrounding Sludgecur. 'Believers in the innocence of Richard III.'

Sludgecur looked at him as if he'd sprouted wings. 'What? This is the Romance of Great Britain you're looking at, mate. Jane Bloody Eyre, Mr Flaming Rochester, Heathcliff and Cathy, Maxim de Winter. Gabriel Oak. This is Love on the Battlefield Day, and we mean to have our money's worth. All right?'

Their money was what it was all about. The fact that they were paying was why Malcolm was here in the first place. But, Jesus, he thought, did these Seekers of Romance even know where they were? Did they know – much less care – that the last King to be killed in armed combat met his fate less than a mile from where they were standing? *And* that he'd met that same fate because of sedition, treachery, and betrayal? Obviously not. They weren't here in support of Richard. They were here because it was part of a package. Love Brooding, Love Hopeless, and Love Devoted had already been checked off the list. And now he was somehow supposed to cook up for them a version of Love Deadly that would make them part with a few quid apiece at the end of the afternoon. Well, all right. He could do that much.

Malcolm didn't think about Betsy until he'd paused at the first marker along the route, which showed King Richard's initial battle position. While his charges took snapshots of the White Boar standard that was whipping in the icy wind from the flagpole marking the King's encampment, Malcolm glanced beyond them to the tumbledown buildings of Windsong Farm, visible at the top of the next hill. He could see the house and he could see Betsy's car in the farmyard. He could imagine – and hope about – the rest.

Bernie wouldn't have noticed that it had taken his wife three and a half hours to purchase a package of minced beef in Market Bosworth. It was nearly half past noon, after all, and doubtless he'd be at the kitchen table where he usually was, attempting to work on yet another of his Formula One models. The pieces would be spread out in front of him and he might have managed to glue one onto the car before the shakes came upon him and he had to have a dose of Black Bush to still them. One dose of whiskey would have led to another until he was too soused to handle a tube of glue.

Chances were good that he'd already passed out onto the model car. It was Saturday and he was supposed to work at St James Church, preparing it for Sunday's service. But poor old Bernie'd have no idea of the day until Betsy returned, slammed the minced beef onto the table next to his ear, and frightened him out of his sodden slumber.

When his head flew up, Betsy would see the imprint of the car's name on his flesh, and she'd be suitably disgusted. Malcolm fresh in her mind, she'd feel the injustice of her position.

'You been to the church yet?' she'd ask Bernie. It was his only job, as no Perryman had farmed the family's land in at least eight generations. 'Father Naughton's not like the others, Bernie. He's not about to put up with you just because you're a Perryman, you know. You got the church *and* the graveyard to see to today. And it's time you were about it.'

Bernie had never been a belligerent drunk, and he wouldn't be one now. He'd say, 'I'm going, sweet Mama. But I got the most godawful thirst. Throat feels like a sandpit, Mama girl.'

He'd smile the same affable smile that had won Betsy's heart in Blackpool where they'd met. And the smile would remind his wife of her duty, despite

Malcolm's ministrations to her earlier. But that was fine, because the last thing that Malcolm Cousins wanted was Betsy Perryman forgetting her duty.

So she'd ask him if he'd taken his medicine, and since Bernie Perryman never did anything – save pour himself a Black Bush – without having been reminded a dozen times, the answer would be no. So Betsy would seek out the pills and shake the dosage into her palm. And Bernie would take it obediently and then stagger out of the house – sans jacket as usual – and head to St James Church to do his duty.

Betsy would call after him to take his jacket, but Bernie would wave off the suggestion. His wife would shout, 'Bernie! You'll catch your death—' and then stop herself at the sudden thought that entered her mind. Bernie's death, after all, was what she needed in order to be with her Beloved.

So her glance would drop to the bottle of pills in her hand and she would read the label: *Digitoxin. Do not exceed one tablet per day without consulting physician.*

Perhaps at that point, she would also hear the doctor's explanation to her: 'It's like digitalis. You've heard of that. An overdose would kill him, Mrs Perryman, so you must be vigilant and see to it that he never takes more than one tablet.'

More than one tablet would ring in her ears. Her morning bonk with Malcolm would live in her memory. She'd shake a pill from the bottle and examine it. She'd finally start to think of a way that the future could be massaged into place.

Happily, Malcolm turned from the farmhouse to his budding Ricardians. All was going according to plan.

'From this location,' Malcolm told his audience of eager but elderly seekers of Love on the Battlefield, 'we can see the village of Sutton Cheney to our northeast.' All heads swivelled in that direction. They may have been freezing their antique pudenda, but at least they were a cooperative group. Save for Sludgecur who, if she had a pudendum, it was no doubt swathed in long underwear. Her expression challenged him to concoct a Romance out of the Battle of Bosworth. Very well, he thought, and picked up the gauntlet. He'd give them Romance. He'd also give them a piece of history that would change their lives. Perhaps this group of Aussie oldies hadn't been Ricardians when they'd arrived at Bosworth Field, but they'd damn well be neophyte Ricardians when they left. *And* they'd return Down Under and tell their grandchildren that it was Malcolm Cousins – *the* Malcolm Cousins, they would say – who had first made them aware of the gross injustice that had been perpetrated upon the memory of a decent King.

'It was there in the village of Sutton Cheney, in St James Church, that King Richard prayed on the night before the battle,' Malcolm told them. 'Picture what the night must have been like.'

From there, he went onto automatic pilot. He'd told the story hundreds of times over the years that he'd served as Special Guide for Groups at Bosworth Field. All he had to do was to milk it for its Romantic Qualities, which wasn't a problem.

The King's forces – 12,000 strong – were encamped on the summit of Ambion Hill where Malcolm Cousins and his band of shivering Neo-Ricardians were standing. The King knew that the morrow would decide his fate: whether he would continue to reign as Richard III or whether his crown would be taken by conquest and worn by an upstart who'd lived most of his life on the Continent, safely tucked away and coddled by those whose ambitions had long been to destroy the York dynasty. The King would have been well aware that his fate rested in the hands of the Stanley brothers: Sir William and Thomas, Lord Stanley. They had arrived at Bosworth with a large army and were encamped to the north, not far from the King, but also – and ominously – not far from the King's pernicious adversary, Henry Tudor, Earl of Richmond, who also happened to be Lord Stanley's stepson. To secure the father's loyalty, King Richard had taken one of Lord Stanley's blood sons as a hostage, the young man's life being the forfeit if his father betrayed England's anointed King by joining Tudor's forces in the upcoming battle. The Stanleys, however, were a wily lot and had shown themselves dedicated to nothing but their own self-interest, so – holding George Stanley hostage or not – the King must have known how great was the risk of entrusting the security of his throne to the whimsies of men whose devotion to self was their most notable quality.

The night before the battle, Richard would have seen the Stanleys camped to the north, in the direction of Market Bosworth. He would have sent a messenger to remind them that, as George Stanley was still being held hostage and as he was being held hostage right there in the King's encampment, the wise course would be to throw their lot in with the King on the morrow.

He would have been restless, Richard. He would have been torn. Having lost first his son and heir and then his wife during his brief reign, having been faced with the treachery of once-close friends, can there be any doubt that he would have wondered – if only fleetingly – how much longer he was meant to go on? And, schooled in the religion of his time, can there be any doubt that he knew how great a sin was despair? And, having established this fact, can there be any question about what the King would have chosen to do on the night before the battle?

Malcolm glanced over his group. Yes, there was a satisfactorily misty eye or two among them. They saw the inherent Romance in a widowed King who'd lost not only his wife but his heir and was hours away from losing his life as well.

Malcolm directed a victorious glance at Sludgecur. Her expression said, Don't press your luck.

It wasn't luck at all, Malcolm wanted to tell her. It was the Great Romance of Hearing the Truth. The wind had picked up velocity and lost another three or four degrees of temperature, but his little band of Antique Aussies were caught in the thrall of that August night in 1485.

The night before the battle, Malcolm told them, knowing that if he lost, he would die, Richard would have sought to be shriven. History tells us that there were no priests or chaplains available among Richard's forces, so what better place to find a confessor than in St James Church. The church would have been quiet as Richard entered. A votive candle or rushlight would have burned in the nave, but nothing more. The only sound inside the building would have come from Richard himself as he moved from the doorway to kneel before the altar: the rustle of his fustian doublet (satin-lined, Malcolm informed his scholars, knowing the importance of detail to the Romantic Minded), the creak of leather from his heavy soled battle shoes and from his scabbard, the clank of his sword and dagger as he—

'Oh my goodness,' a Romantic Neo-Ricardian chirruped. 'What sort of man would take swords and daggers into a church?'

Malcolm smiled winsomely. He thought, A man who had a bloody good use for them, just the very things needed for a bloke who wanted to prise loose a stone. But what he said was, 'Unusual, of course. One doesn't think of someone carrying weapons into a church, does one? But this was the night before the battle. Richard's enemies were everywhere. He wouldn't have walked into the darkness unprotected.'

Whether the King wore his crown that night into the church, no one can say, Malcolm continued. But if there was a priest in the church to hear his confession, that same priest left Richard to his prayers soon after giving him absolution. And there in the darkness, lit only by the small rushlight in the nave, Richard made peace with his Lord God and prepared to meet the fate that the next day's battle promised him.

Malcolm eyed his audience, gauging their reactions and their attentiveness. They were entirely with him. They were, he hoped, thinking about how much they should tip him for giving a bravura performance in the deadly wind.

His prayers finished, Malcolm informed them, the King unsheathed his sword and dagger, set them on the rough wooden bench, and sat next to them. And there in the church, King Richard laid his plans to ruin Henry Tudor should the upstart be the victor in the morrow's battle. Because Richard knew that he held – and had always held – the whip hand over Henry Tudor. He held it in life as a proven and victorious battle commander. He would hold it in death as the single force who could destroy the usurper.

'Goodness me,' someone murmured appreciatively. Yes, Malcolm's listeners were fully attuned to the Romance of the Moment. Thank God.

Richard, he told them, wasn't oblivious of the scheming that had been going on between Henry

Tudor and Elizabeth Woodville – widow of his brother Edward IV and mother of the two young Princes whom he had earlier placed in the Tower of London.

'The Princes in the Tower,' another voice remarked. 'That's the two little boys who—'

'The very ones,' Malcolm said solemnly. 'Richard's own nephews.'

The King would have known that, holding true to her propensity for buttering her bread not only on both sides but along the crust as well, Elizabeth Woodville had promised the hand of her eldest daughter to Tudor should he obtain the crown of England. But should Tudor obtain the crown of England on the morrow, Richard also knew that every man, woman, and child with a drop of York blood in his body stood in grave danger of being eliminated – permanently – as a claimant to the throne. And this included Elizabeth Woodville's children.

He himself ruled by right of succession and by law. Descended directly – and more important legitimately from Edward III – he had come to the throne

after the death of his brother Edward IV, upon the revelation of the licentious Edward's secret pledge of marriage to another woman long before his marriage to Elizabeth Woodville. This pledged contract of marriage had been made before a bishop of the church. As such, it was as good as a marriage performed with pomp and circumstance before a thousand onlookers, and it effectively made Edward's later marriage to Elizabeth Woodville bigamous at the same time as it bastardized all of their children.

Henry Tudor would have known that the children had been declared illegitimate by an Act of Parliament. He would also have known that, should he be victorious in his confrontation with Richard III, his tenuous claim to the throne of England would not be shored up by marriage to the bastard daughter of a dead King. So he would have to do something about her illegitimacy.

King Richard would have concluded this once he heard the news that Tudor had pledged to marry the girl. He would also have known that to legitimatize Elizabeth of York was also to legitimatize all her sisters . . . and her brothers. One could not declare the eldest child of a dead King legitimate while simultaneously claiming her siblings were not.

Malcolm paused meaningfully in his narrative. He waited to see if the eager Romantics gathered round him would twig the implication. They smiled and nodded and looked at him fondly, but no one said anything. So Malcolm did their twigging for them.

'Her brothers,' he said patiently, and slowly to make sure they absorbed each Romantic detail. 'If Henry Tudor legitimatized Elizabeth of York prior to marrying her, he would have been legitimatising her brothers as well. And if he did that, the elder of the boys—'

'Gracious me,' one of the group sang out. '*He* would've been the true King once Richard died.'

Bless you, my child, Malcolm thought. 'That,' he cried, 'is exactly spot on.'

'See here, mate,' Sludgecur interrupted, some sort of light dawning in the cobwebbed reaches of her brain. 'I've heard this story, and Richard killed those little blighters himself while they were in the Tower.'

Another fish biting the Tudor bait, Malcolm realized. Five hundred years later and that scheming

Welsh upstart was still successfully reeling them in. He could hardly wait until the day when his book came out, when his history of Richard was heralded as the triumph of truth over Tudor casuistry.

He was Patience itself as he explained. The Princes in the Tower – Edward IV's two sons – had indeed been long reputed by tradition to have been murdered by their uncle Richard III to shore up his position as King. But there were no witnesses to any murder and as Richard was King through an Act of Parliament, he had no motive to kill them. And since he had no direct heir to the throne – his own son having died, as you heard moments ago – what better way to ensure the Yorks' continued possession of the throne of England than to designate the two Princes legitimate . . . after his own death? Such designation could only be made by Papal decree at this point, but Richard had sent two emissaries to Rome and why send them such a distance unless it was to arrange for the legitimatizing of the very boys whose rights had been wrested from them by their father's lascivious conduct?

'The boys were indeed rumoured to be dead,'

Malcolm aimed for kindness in his tone. 'But that rumour, interestingly enough, never saw the light of day until just before Henry Tudor's invasion of England. He wanted to be King, but he had no rights to kingship. So he had to discredit the reigning monarch. Could there possibly be a more efficacious way to do it than by spreading the word that the Princes – who were gone from the Tower – were actually dead? But this is the question I pose to you, ladies: What if they weren't?'

An appreciative murmur went through the group. Malcolm heard one of the ancients commenting, 'Lovely eyes, he has', and he turned them towards the sound of her voice. She looked like his grandmother. She also looked rich. He increased the wattage of his charm.

'What if the two boys had been removed from the Tower by Richard's own hand, sent into safe-keeping against a possible uprising? Should Henry Tudor prevail at Bosworth Field, those two boys would be in grave danger and King Richard knew it. Tudor was pledged to their sister. To marry her, he had to declare her legitimate. Declaring her legitimate made them legitimate. Making them legitimate made one of them – young Edward – the true and rightful King of England. The only way for Tudor to prevent this was to get rid of them. Permanently.'

Malcolm waited a moment to let this sink in. He noted the collection of grey heads turning towards Sutton Cheney. Then towards the north valley where a flagpole flew the seditious Stanleys' standard. Then over towards the peak of Ambion Hill where the unforgiving wind whipped Richard's White Boar briskly. Then down the slope in the direction of the railway tracks where the Tudor mercenaries had once formed their meagre front line. Vastly outnumbered, outgunned, and outarmed, they would have been waiting for the Stanleys to make their move: for King Richard or against him. Without the Stanleys' throwing their lot in with Tudor's, the day would be lost.

The Grey Ones were clearly with him, Malcolm noted. But Sludgecur was not so easily drawn in. 'How was Tudor supposed to kill them if they were gone from the Tower?' She'd taken to beating her hands against her arms, doubtless wishing she were pummelling his face.

'He didn't kill them,' Malcolm said pleasantly, 'although his Machiavellian fingerprints are all over the crime. No. Tudor wasn't directly involved. I'm afraid the situation's a little nastier than that. Shall we walk on and discuss it, ladies?'

'Lovely little bum as well,' one of the group murmured. 'Quite a crumpet, that bloke.'

Ah, they were in his palm. Malcolm felt himself warm to his own seductive talents.

He knew that Betsy was watching from the farmhouse, from the first floor bedroom from which she could see the battlefield. How could she possibly keep herself from doing so after their morning together? She'd see Malcolm shepherding his little band from site to site, she'd note that they were hanging onto his every word, and she'd think about how she herself had hung upon him less than two hours earlier. And the contrast between her drunken sot of a husband and her virile lover would be painfully and mightily on her mind.

This would make her realize how wasted she was on Bernie Perryman. She was, she would think, forty years old and at the prime of her life. She deserved better than Bernie. She deserved, in fact, a man who understood God's plan when He'd created the first man and woman. He'd used the man's rib, hadn't He? In doing that, He'd illustrated for all time that women and men were bound together, women taking their form and substance from their men, living their lives in the service of their men for which their reward was to be sheltered and protected by their men's superior strength. But Bernie Perryman only ever saw one half of the man-woman equation. She – Betsy – was to work in his service, care for him, feed him, see to his wellbeing. He – Bernie – was to do nothing. Oh, he'd make a feeble attempt to give her a length now and again if the mood was upon him and he could keep it up long enough. But whiskey had long since robbed him of whatever ability he'd once had to be pleasing to a woman. And as for understanding her subtler needs and his responsibility in meeting them . . . forget that area of life altogether.

I, Richard

Malcolm liked to think of Betsy in these terms: up in her barren bedroom in the farmhouse, nursing a righteous grievance against her husband. She would proceed from that grievance to the realisation that he, Malcolm Cousins, was the man she'd been intended for, and she would see how every other relationship in her life had been but a prologue to the connection she now had with him. She and Malcolm, she would conclude, were suited for each other in every way.

Watching him on the battlefield, she would recall their initial meeting and the fire that had existed between them from the first day when Betsy had begun to work at Gloucester Grammar as the Headmaster's Secretary. She'd recall the spark she'd felt when Malcolm had said, 'Bernie Perryman's wife?' and admired her openly. 'Old Bernie's been holding back on me, and I thought we shared every secret of our souls.' She would remember how she'd asked, 'You know Bernie?' still in the blush of her newlywed bliss and not yet aware of how Bernie's drinking was going to impair his ability to care for her. And she'd well remember Malcolm's response: 'Have done for years. We grew up together, went to school together,

◦

91

spent holidays roaming the countryside. We even shared our first woman—' and she'd remember his smile – 'so we're practically blood brothers if it comes to that. But I can see there might be a decided impediment to our future relationship, Betsy.' And his eyes had held hers just long enough for her to realize that her newlywed bliss wasn't nearly as hot as the look he was giving her.

From that upstairs bedroom, she'd see that the group Malcolm was squiring round the field comprised women, and she'd begin to worry. The distance from the farmhouse to the field would prevent her from seeing that Malcolm's antiquated audience had one collective foot in the collective grave, so her thoughts would turn ineluctably to the possibilities implied by his current circumstances. What was to prevent one of those women from becoming captivated by the enchantment he offered?

These thoughts would lead to her desperation, which was what Malcolm had been assiduously massaging for months, whispering at the most tender of moments, 'Oh God, if I'd only known what it was going to be like to have you, finally. And now to want you completely . . .' And then the tears, wept into her hair, and the revelation of the agonies of guilt and despair he experienced each time he rolled deliciously within the arms of his old friend's wife. 'I can't bear to hurt him, darling Bets. If you and he were to divorce . . . How could I ever live with myself if he ever knew how I've betrayed our friendship?'

She'd remember this, in the farmhouse bedroom with her hot forehead pressed to the cold window-pane. They'd been together for three hours that morning, but she'd realize that it was not enough. It would never be enough to sneak round as they were doing, to pretend indifference to each other when they met at Gloucester Grammar. Until they were a couple – legally, as much as they were already a couple spiritually, mentally, emotionally, and physically – she could never have peace.

But Bernie stood between her and happiness, she would think. Bernie Perryman, driven to alcohol by the demon of fear that the congenital abnormality that had taken his grandfather, his father, and both of his brothers before their forty-fifth birthdays would claim him as well. 'Weak heart,' Bernie had doubtless told her, since he'd used it as an excuse for everything he'd done – and not done – for the last thirty years. 'It don't ever pump like it ought. Just a little flutter when it oughter be a thud. Got to be careful. Got to take m' pills.'

But if Betsy didn't remind her husband to take his pills daily, he was likely to forget there were pills altogether, let alone a reason for taking them. It was almost as if he had a death wish, Bernie Perryman. It was almost as if he was only waiting for the appropriate moment to set her free.

And once she was free, Betsy would think, The Legacy would be hers. And The Legacy was the key to her future with Malcolm. Because with The Legacy in hand at last, she and Malcolm could marry and Malcolm could leave his ill-paying job at Gloucester Grammar. Content with his research, his writing, and his lecturing, he would be filled with gratitude for her having made his new lifestyle possible. Grateful, he would be eager to meet her needs.

Which is, she would think, certainly how it was meant to be.

*   *   *

I, Richard

In the Plantagenet pub in Sutton Cheney, Malcolm counted the tip money from his morning's labour. He'd given his all, but the Aussie Oldies had proved to be a niggardly lot. He'd ended up with forty pounds for the tour and lecture – which was an awesomely cheap price considering the depth of information he imparted – and twenty-five pounds in tips. Thank God for the pound coin, he concluded morosely. Without it, the tightfisted old sluts would probably have parted with nothing more than fifty pence apiece.

He pocketed the money as the pub door opened and a gust of icy air whooshed into the room. The flames of the fire next to him bobbled. Ash from the fireplace blew onto the hearth. Malcolm looked up. Bernie Perryman – clad only in cowboy boots, blue jeans, and a T-shirt with the words *Team Ferrari* printed on it – staggered drunkenly into the pub. Malcolm tried to shrink out of view, but it was impossible. After the prolonged exposure to the wind on Bosworth Field, his need for warmth had taken him to the blazing beechwood fire. This put him directly in Bernie's sightline.

'Malkie!' Bernie cried out joyfully, and went on as he always did whenever they met. 'Malkie ol' mate! How 'bout a chess game? I miss our matches, I surely do.' He shivered and beat his hands against his arms. His lips were practically blue. 'Shit on toast. It's blowing a cold one out there. Pour me a Blackie,' he called out to the publican. 'Make it a double and make it double quick.' He grinned and dropped onto the stool at Malcolm's table. 'So. How's the book comin', Malkie? Gotcher name in lights? Found a publisher yet?' He giggled.

Malcolm put aside whatever guilt he may have felt at the fact that he was industriously stuffing this inebriate's wife whenever his middle-aged body was up to the challenge. Bernie Perryman deserved to be a cuckold, his punishment for the torment he'd been dishing out to Malcolm for the last ten years.

'Never got over that last game, did you?' Bernie grinned again. He was served his Black Bush which he tossed back in a single gulp. He blubbered air out between his lips. He said, 'Did me right, that,' and called for another. 'Now what was the full-on tale again, Malkie? You get to the good part of the story yet? 'Course, it'll be a tough one to prove, won't it, mate?'

Malcolm counted to ten. Bernie was presented with his second double whiskey. It went the way of the first.

'But I'm givin' you a bad time for nothing,' Bernie said, suddenly repentant in the way of all drunks. 'You never did me a bad turn – 'cept that time with the A levels, 'course – and I shouldn't do you one. I wish you the best. Truly, I do. It's just that things never work out the way they're s'posed to, do they?'

Which, Malcolm thought, was the whole bloody point. Things – as Bernie liked to call them – hadn't worked out for Richard either, that fatal morning on Bosworth Field. The Earl of Northumberland had let him down, the Stanleys had out-and-out betrayed him, and an untried upstart who had neither the skill nor the courage to face the King personally in decisive combat had won the day.

'So tell Bern your theory another time. I love the story, I do, I do. I just wished there was a way for you to prove it. It'd be the making of you, that book would. How long you been working on the manuscript?' Bernie swiped the interior of his whiskey glass with a dirty finger and licked off the residue. He wiped his mouth on the back of his hand. He hadn't shaved that morning. He hadn't bathed in days. For a moment, Malcolm almost felt sorry for Betsy, having to live in the same house with the odious man.

'I've come to Elizabeth of York,' Malcolm said as pleasantly as he could manage, considering the antipathy he was feeling for Bernie. 'Edward IV's daughter. Future wife to the King of England.'

Bernie smiled, showing teeth in serious need of cleaning. 'Cor, I always forget that bird, Malkie. Why's that, d'you think?'

Because everyone always forgot Elizabeth, Malcolm said silently. The eldest daughter of Edward IV, she was generally consigned to a footnote in history as the oldest sister of the Princes in the Tower, the dutiful daughter of Elizabeth Woodville, a pawn in the political power game, the later wife of that Tudor usurper Henry VII. Her job was to carry the seed of the dynasty, to deliver the heirs, and to fade into obscurity.

But here was a woman who was one-half Woodville, with the thick blood of that scheming and ambitious clan coursing through her veins. That she wanted to be Queen of England like her mother before her had been established in the seventeenth century when Sir George Buck had written – in his *History of the Life and Reigne of Richard III* – of young Elizabeth's letter asking the Duke of Norfolk to be the mediator between herself and King Richard on the subject of their marriage, telling him that she was the King's in heart and in thought. That she was as ruthless as her two parents was made evident in the fact that her letter to Norfolk was written prior to the death of Richard's wife, Queen Anne.

Young Elizabeth had been bundled out of London and up to Yorkshire, ostensibly for safety's sake, prior to Henry Tudor's invasion. There she resided at Sheriff Hutton, a stronghold deep in the country-side where loyalty to King Richard was a constant of life. Elizabeth would be well-protected – not to mention well-guarded – in Yorkshire. As would be her siblings.

'You still hot for Lizzie?' Bernie asked with

a chuckle. 'Cor, how you used to go on about that girl.'

Malcolm suppressed his rage but did not forbid himself from silently cursing the other man into eternal torment. Bernie had a deep aversion for anyone who tried to make something of his life. That sort of person served to remind him of what a waste he'd made of his own.

Bernie must have read something on Malcolm's face because as he called for his third double whiskey, he said, 'No, no, get on with you. I 'as only kidding. What's you doing out here today anyway? Was that you in the battlefield when I drove by?'

Bernie knew it was he, Malcolm realized. But mentioning the fact served to remind them both of Malcolm's passion and the hold that Bernie Perryman had upon it. God, how he wanted to stand on the table and shout, 'I'm bonking this idiot's wife twice a week, three or four times if I can manage it. They'd been married two months when I bonked her the first time, six days after we were introduced.'

I, Richard

But losing control like that was exactly what Bernie Perryman wanted of his old friend Malcolm Cousins: payback time for having once refused to help Bernie cheat his way through his A-levels. The man had an elephantine memory and a grudge-bearing spirit. But so did Malcolm.

'I don't know, Malkie,' Bernie said, shaking his head as he was presented with his whiskey. He reached unsteadily for it, his bloodless tongue wetting his lower lip. 'Don't seem natural that Lizzie'd hand those lads over to be given the chop. Not her own brothers. Not even to be Queen of England. Sides, they weren't even anywheres near her, were they? All speculation, 'f you ask me. All speculation and not a speck of proof.'

Never, Malcolm thought for the thousandth time, never tell a drunkard your secrets or your dreams.

'It was Elizabeth of York,' he said again. 'She was ultimately responsible.'

Sheriff Hutton was not an insurmountable distance from Rievaulx, Jervaulx, and Fountains Abbeys. And tucking individuals away in abbeys, convents, monasteries, and priories was a great tradition at that time. Women were the usual recipients of a one-way ticket to the ascetic life. But two young boys – disguised as youthful entrants into a novitiate – would have been safe there from the arm of Henry Tudor should he take the throne of England by means of conquest.

'Tudor would have known the boys were alive,' Malcolm said. 'When he pledged himself to marry Elizabeth, he would have known the boys were alive.'

Bernie nodded. 'Poor little tykes,' he said with factitious sorrow. 'And poor old Richard who took the blame. How'd she get her mitts on them, Malkie? What d'you think? Think she cooked up a deal with Tudor?'

'She wanted to be a Queen more than she wanted to be merely the sister to a King. There was only one way to make that happen. And Henry had been looking elsewhere for a wife at the same time that he was bargaining with Elizabeth Woodville. The girl would have known that. And what it meant.'

Bernie nodded solemnly, as if he cared a half fig for what had happened more than five hundred years ago on an August night not two hundred yards from the pub in which they sat. He shot back his third double whiskey and slapped his stomach like a man at the end of a hearty meal.

'Got the church all prettied up for tomorrow,' he informed Malcolm. ''Mazing when you think of it, Malkie. Perrymans been tinkering round St James Church for two hundred years. Like a family pedigree, that. Don't you think? Remarkable, I'd say.'

Malcolm regarded him evenly. 'Utterly remarkable, Bernie,' he said.

'Ever think how different life might've been if your dad and granddad and his granddad before him were the ones who tinkered round St James Church? P'rhaps I'd be you and you'd be me. What d'you think of that?'

What Malcolm thought of that couldn't be spoken to the man sitting opposite him at the table. Die, he thought. Die before I kill you myself.

'Do you want to be together, darling?' Betsy breathed the question wetly into his ear. Another Saturday. Another three hours of bonking Betsy. Malcolm wondered how much longer he'd have to continue with the charade.

He wanted to ask her to move over – the woman was capable of inducing claustrophobia with more efficacy than a plastic bag – but at this point in their relationship he knew that a demonstration of post-coital togetherness was as important to his ultimate objective as was a top-notch performance between the sheets. And since his age, his inclinations, and his energy were all combining to take his performances down a notch each time he sank between Betsy's well-padded thighs, he realized the wisdom of allowing her to cling, coo, and cuddle for as long as he could endure it without screaming once the primal act was completed between them.

'We *are* together,' he said, stroking her hair. It was wire-like to the touch, the result of too much bleaching and even more hair spray. 'Unless you mean that you want another go. And I'll need some recovery time for that.' He turned his head and pressed his lips to her forehead. 'You take it out of me and that's the truth of it, darling Bets. You're woman enough for a dozen men.'

She giggled. 'You love it.'

'Not it. You. Love, want, and can't be without.' He sometimes pondered where he came up with the nonsense he told her. It was as if a primitive part of his brain reserved for female seduction went onto autopilot whenever Betsy climbed into his bed.

She buried her fingers in his ample chest hair. 'I mean really be together, darling. Do you want it? The two of us? Like this? Forever? Do you want it more than anything on earth?'

The thought alone was like being imprisoned in concrete. But he said, 'Darling Bets,' by way of answer and he trembled his voice appropriately. 'Don't. Please. We can't go through this again.' And he pulled her roughly to him because he knew that was the move she desired. He sank his face into the curve of her shoulder and neck. He breathed through his mouth to avoid inhaling the day's litre of Shalimar that she'd doused herself with. He made the whimpering noises of a man *in extremis*. God, what he wouldn't do for King Richard.

'I was on the Internet,' she whispered, fingers

caressing the back of his neck. 'In the school library. All Thursday and Friday lunch, darling.'

He stopped his whimpering, sifting through this declaration for deeper meaning. 'Were you?' He temporised by nibbling at her ear lobe, waiting for more information. It came obliquely.

'You *do* love me, don't you, Malcolm dearest?'

'What do you think?'

'And you do want me, don't you?'

'That's obvious, isn't it?'

'Forever and ever?'

Whatever it takes, he thought. And he did his best to prove it to her, although his body wasn't up to a full performance.

Afterwards, while she was dressing, she said, 'I was so surprised to see all the topics. You c'n look up anything on the Internet. Fancy that, Malcolm. Anything at all. Bernie's playing in chess night at the Plantagenet, dearest. Tonight, that is.'

Malcolm furrowed his brow, automatically seeking the connection between these apparently unrelated topics. She went on.

'He misses your games, Bernie does. He always

wishes you'd come by on chess night and give it another go with him, darling.' She padded to the chest of drawers where she began repairing her make-up. ''Course, he doesn't play well. Just uses chess as an extra excuse to go to the pub.'

Malcolm watched her, eyes narrowed, waiting for a sign.

She gave it to him. 'I worry about him, Malcolm dear. His poor heart's going to give out someday. I'm going with him tonight. Perhaps we'll see you there? Malcolm, dearest, do you love me? Do you want to be together more than anything on earth?'

He saw that she was watching him closely in the mirror even as she repaired the damage he'd done to her make-up. She was painting her lips into bee-stung bows. She was brushing her cheeks with blusher. But all the time she was observing him.

'More than life itself,' he said.

And when she smiled, he knew he'd given her the correct answer.

That night at the Plantagenet pub, Malcolm joined

the Sutton Cheney Chessmen, of whose society he'd once been a regular member. Bernie Perryman was delighted to see him. He deserted his regular opponent – seventy-year-old Angus Ferguson who used the excuse of playing chess at the Plantagenet to get as sloshed as Bernie – and pressed Malcolm into a game at a table in the smoky corner of the pub. Betsy was right, naturally: Bernie drank far more than he played, and the Black Bush served to oil the mechanism of his conversation. So he also talked incessantly.

He talked to Betsy, who was playing the role of serving-wench for her husband that evening. From half past seven until half past ten, she trotted back and forth from the bar, bringing Bernie one double Black Bush after another, saying, 'You're drinking too much,' and 'This is the last one, Bernie,' in a monitory fashion. But he always managed to talk her into 'just one more wet one, Mama girl', and he patted her bum, winked at Malcolm and whispered loudly what he intended to do to her once he got her home. Malcolm was at the point of thinking he'd utterly misunderstood Betsy's implied message to him in bed that morning when she finally made her move.

It came at half past ten, one hour before George the Publican called for last orders. The pub was packed, and Malcolm might have missed her manoeuvre altogether had he not anticipated that something was going to happen that night. As Bernie nodded over the chessboard, contemplating his next move eternally, Betsy went to the bar for yet another 'double Blackie'. To do this, she had to shoulder her way through the Sutton Cheney Dartsmen, the Wardens of the Church, a women's support group from Dadlington, and a group of teenagers intent upon success with a fruit machine. She paused in conversation with a balding woman who seemed to be admiring Betsy's hair with that sort of artificial enthusiasm women reserve for other women whom they particularly hate, and it was while she and the other chatted that Malcolm saw her empty the vial into Bernie's tumbler.

He was awestruck at the ease with which she did it. She must have been practising the move for days, he realized. She was so adept that she did it with one hand as she chatted: slipping the vial out of her sweater sleeve, uncapping it, dumping it, returning it to her sweater. She finished her conversation, and she continued on her way. And no one save Malcolm was wise to the fact that she'd done something more than merely fetch another whiskey for her husband. Malcolm eyed her with new respect when she set the glass in front of Bernie. He was glad he had no intention of hooking himself up with the murderous bitch.

He knew what was in the glass: the results of Betsy's few hours surfing the Internet. She'd crushed at least ten tablets of Digitoxin into a lethal powder. An hour after Bernie ingested the mixture, he'd be a dead man.

Ingest it Bernie did. He drank it down the way he drank down every double Black Bush he encountered: he poured it directly down his throat and wiped his mouth on the back of his hand. Malcolm had lost count of the number of whiskeys Bernie had imbibed that evening, but it seemed to him that if the drug didn't kill him, the alcohol certainly would.

'Bernie,' Betsy said mournfully, 'let's go home.'

'Can't just yet,' Bernie said. 'Got to finish my bit with Malkie boy here. We haven't had us a chess-up in years. Not since . . .' He smiled at Malcolm blearily. 'Why, I 'member that night up the farm, doanchew, Malkie? Ten years back? Longer was it? When we played that last game, you and me?'

Malcolm didn't want to get onto that subject. He said, 'Your move, Bernie. Or do you want to call it a draw?'

'No way, Joe-zay.' Bernie swayed on his stool and studied the board.

'Bernie . . .' Betsy said coaxingly.

He patted her hand, which she'd laid on his shoulder. 'You g'wan, Bets. I c'n find my way home. Malkie'll drive me, woanchew, Malkie?' He dug his car keys out of his pocket and pressed them into his wife's palm. 'But doanchew fall asleep, sweet Mama. We got business together when I get home.'

Betsy made a show of reluctance and a secondary show of her concern that Malcolm might have had too much to drink himself and thereby be an unsafe driver for her precious Bernie to ride along with. Bernie said, ''F he can't do a straight line in the car park, I'll walk. Promise, Mama. Cross m' heart.'

Betsy levelled a meaningful look at Malcolm. She said, 'See that you keep him safe, then.'

Malcolm nodded. Betsy departed. and all that was left was the waiting.

For someone who was supposed to be suffering from congenital heart failure, Bernie Perryman seemed to have the constitution of a mule. An hour later, Malcolm had him in the car and was driving him home, and Bernie was still talking like a man with a new lease on life. He was just itching to get up those farmhouse stairs and rip off his wife's knickers, to hear him tell it. Nothing but the Day of Judgement was going to stop Bernie from showing his Sweet Mama the time of her life.

By the time Malcolm had taken the longest route possible to get to the farm without raising Bernie's suspicions, he'd begun to believe that his paramour hadn't slipped her husband an overdose of his medication at all. It was only when Bernie got out of the car at the edge of the drive that Malcolm had his hopes renewed. Bernie said, 'Feel peaked a bit, Malkie. Whew. Nice lie down. Tha's just the ticket', and staggered in the direction of the distant house. Malcolm watched him until he toppled into the hedgerow at the side of the drive. When he didn't move after the fall, Malcolm knew that the deed had finally been done.

He drove off happily. If Bernie hadn't been dead when he hit the ground, Malcolm knew that he'd be dead by the morning.

Wonderful, he thought. It may have been ages in the execution, but his well laid plan was going to pay off.

Malcolm had worried a bit that Betsy might muff her role in the ensuing drama. But during the next few days, she proved herself to be an actress of formidable talents. Having awakened in the morning to discover herself alone in the bed, she'd done what any sensible wife-of-a-drunk would do: she went looking for her husband. She didn't find him anywhere in the house or in the other farm buildings, so she placed a few phone calls. She checked the pub;

she checked the church; she checked with Malcolm. Had Malcolm not seen her poison her husband with his own eyes, he would have been convinced that on the other end of the line was a woman anxious for the welfare of her man. But then, she *was* anxious, wasn't she? She needed a corpse to prove Bernie was dead.

'I dropped him at the end of the drive,' Malcolm told her, help and concern personified. 'He was heading up to the house the last I saw him, Bets.'

So out she went and found Bernie exactly where he'd fallen on the previous night. And her discovery of his body set the necessary events in motion.

An inquest was called, of course. But it proved to be a mere formality. Bernie's history of heart problems and his 'difficulty with the drink', as the authorities put it, combined with the fiercely inclement weather they'd been having to provide the coroner's jury with a most reasonable conclusion. Bernie Perryman was declared dead of exposure, having passed out on the coldest night of the year, teetering up the lengthy drive to the farmhouse after a full night of drink at the Plantagenet pub, where sixteen witnesses called to testify had seen him down at least eleven double whiskeys in less than three hours.

There was no reason to check for toxicity in his blood. Especially once his doctor said that it was a miracle the man had lived to forty-nine, considering the medical history of his family, not to mention his 'problem with the drink'.

So Bernie was buried at the side of his forebears, in the graveyard of St James Church, where his father and all the fathers before him for at least the past two hundred years had toiled in the cause of a neat and tidy house of worship.

Malcolm soothed what few pangs of guilt he had over Bernie's passing by ignoring them. Bernie'd had a history of heart disease. Bernie had been a notorious drunk. If Bernie, in his cups, had passed out on the driveway a mere fifty yards from his house and died from exposure as a result . . . well, who could possibly hold himself responsible?

And while it was sad that Bernie Perryman had had to give his life for the cause of Malcolm's search for the truth, it was also the truth that he'd brought his premature death upon himself.

After the funeral, Malcolm knew that all he needed to employ was patience. He hadn't spent the last two years industriously ploughing Betsy's field, only to be thwarted by a display of unseemly haste at the moment of harvest. Besides, Betsy was doing enough bit chomping for both of them, so he knew it was only a matter of days – perhaps hours – before she took herself off to the Perrymans' longtime solicitor for an accounting of the inheritance that was coming her way.

Malcolm had pictured the moment enough times during his liaison with Betsy. Sometimes picturing the moment when Betsy learned the truth was the only fantasy that got him through his interminable lovemaking sessions with the woman.

Howard Smythe-Thomas would open his Nuneaton office to her and break the news in a suitably funereal fashion, no doubt. And perhaps at first, Betsy would think his sombre demeanour was an air adopted for the occasion. He'd begin by calling her 'My dear Mrs

Perryman', which should give her an idea that bad news was in the offing, but she wouldn't have an inkling of how bad the news was until he spelled out the bitter reality for her.

Bernie had no money. The farm had been mortgaged three times; there were no savings worth speaking of and no investments. The contents of the house and the outbuildings were hers, of course, but only by selling off every possession – and the farm itself – would Betsy be able to avoid bankruptcy. And even then, it would be touch and go. The only reason the bank hadn't foreclosed on the property before now was that the Perrymans had been doing business with that same financial institution for more than two hundred years. 'Loyalty,' Mr Smythe-Thomas would no doubt intone. 'Bernard may have had his difficulties, Mrs Perryman, but the bank had respect for his lineage. When one's father and one's father's father and his father before him have done business with a banking establishment, there is a certain leeway given that might not be given to a personage less well known to that bank.'

117

Which would be legal doublespeak for the fact that since there were no other Perrymans at Windsong Farm – and Mr Smythe-Thomas would be good about gently explaining that a short-term wife of a long-term alcoholic Perryman didn't count – the bank would probably be calling in Bernie's debts. She would be wise to prepare herself for that eventuality.

But what about The Legacy? Betsy would ask. 'Bernie always nattered on about a legacy.' And she would be stunned to think of the depth of her husband's deception.

Mr Smythe-Thomas, naturally, would know nothing about a legacy. And considering the Perryman history of ne'er-do-wells earning their keep by doing nothing more than working round the church in Sutton Cheney . . . He would kindly point out that it wasn't very likely that anyone had managed to amass a fortune doing handywork, was it?

It would take some hours – perhaps even days – for the news to sink into Betsy's skull. She'd think at first that there had to be some sort of mistake. Surely there were jewels hidden somewhere, cash tucked away, silver or gold or deeds to property heretofore unknown packed in the attic. And thinking this, she would begin her search. Which was exactly what Malcolm intended her to do: search first and come weeping to Malcolm second. And Malcolm himself would take it from there.

In the meantime, he happily worked on his magnum opus. The pages to the left of his typewriter piled up satisfactorily as he redeemed the reputation of England's most maligned King.

Many of the righteous fell that morning of 22 August 1485, and among them was the Duke of Norfolk, who commanded the vanguard at the front of Richard's army. When the Earl of Northumberland refused to engage his forces to come to the aid of Norfolk's leaderless men, the psychological tide of the battle shifted.

Those were the days of mass desertions, of switching loyalties, of outright betrayals on the field of battle. And both the King and his Tudor foe would have known that. Which went far to explain why both men simultaneously needed and doubted the Stanleys. Which also went far to explain why – in the midst of the battle – Henry Tudor made a run for the Stanleys, who had so far refused to enter the fray. Outnumbered as he was, Henry Tudor's cause would be lost without the Stanleys' intervention. And he wasn't above begging for it, which is why he made that desperate ride across the plain towards the Stanley forces.

King Richard intercepted him, thundering down Ambion Hill with his Knights and Esquires of the Body. The two small forces engaged each other a bare half mile from the Stanleys' men. Tudor's knights began falling quickly under the King's attack: William Brandon and the banner of Cadwallader plummeted to the ground; the enormous Sir John Cheyney fell beneath the King's own axe. It was only a matter of moments before Richard might fight his way to Henry Tudor himself, which was what the Stanleys realized when they made their decision to attack the King's small force.

In the ensuing battle, King Richard was unhorsed and could have fled the field. But declaring that he would 'die King of England', he continued to fight even when grievously wounded. It took more than one man to bring him down. And he died like the Royal Prince that he was.

The King's army fled, pursued hotly by the Earl of Oxford whose intent it would have been to kill as many of them as possible. They shot off towards the village of Stoke Golding, in the opposite direction from Sutton Cheney.

This fact was the crux of the events that followed. When one's life is hanging in the balance, when one is a blood relative of the defeated King of England, one's thoughts turn inexorably towards self-preservation. John de la Pole, Earl of Lincoln and nephew to King Richard, was among the fleeing forces. To ride towards Sutton Cheney would have put him directly into the clutches of the Earl of Northumberland who had refused to come to the King's aid and would have been only too happy to cement his position in Henry Tudor's affections – such as they were – by handing over the dead King's nephew. So he rode to the south instead of to the north. And in doing so, he condemned his uncle to five hundred years of Tudor propaganda.

Because history is written by the winners, Malcolm thought.

Only sometimes history gets to be rewritten.

And as he rewrote it, in the back of his mind was the picture of Betsy and her growing desperation. In the two weeks following Bernie's death, she hadn't returned to work. Gloucester Grammar's Headmaster – the snivelling Samuel, as Malcolm liked to call him – reported that Betsy was prostrate over her husband's sudden death. She needed time to deal with and to heal from her grief, he told the staff sorrowfully.

Malcolm knew that what she had to deal with was finding something that she could pass off as The Legacy so as to bind him to her despite the fact that her expectations of inheritance had come to nothing. Tearing through the old farmhouse like a wild thing, she would probably go through Bernie's wardrobe one thread at a time in an attempt to unearth some item of value. She'd shake open books, seeking everything from treasure maps to deeds. She'd sift through the contents of the half dozen trunks in the attic. She'd knock about the outbuildings with her lips turning blue from the cold. And if she was assiduous, she would find the key.

And the key would take her to the safe deposit box at that very same bank in which the Perrymans had transacted business for two hundred years. Widow of Bernard Perryman with his will in one hand and his death certificate in the other, she would be given access. And there, she'd come to the end of her hopes.

Malcolm wondered what she would think when she saw the single grubby piece of paper that was the long heralded Legacy of the Perrymans. Filled with handwriting so cramped as to be virtually illegible, it looked like nothing to the untrained eye. And that's what Betsy would think she had in her possession when she finally threw herself upon Malcolm's mercy.

Bernie Perryman had known otherwise, however, on that long ago night when he'd shown Malcolm the letter.

'Have a lookit this here, Malkie,' Bernie had said. 'Tell ol' Bern whatchoo think of this.'

He was in his cups, as usual, but he wasn't yet entirely blotto. And Malcolm, having just obliterated him at chess, was feeling expansive and willing to put up with his childhood friend's inebriated ramblings.

At first he thought that Bernie was taking a page from out of a large old Bible, but he quickly saw that the Bible was really an antique leather album of some sort and the page was a document, a letter in fact. Although it had no salutation, it was signed at the bottom and next to the signature was the remains of a wax imprint from a signet ring.

Bernie was watching him in that sly way drunks have: gauging his reaction. So Malcolm knew that Bernie knew what it was that he had in his possession. Which made him curious, but wary as well.

The wary part of him glanced at the document, saying, 'I don't know, Bernie. I can't make much of it.' While the curious part of him added, 'Where'd it come from?'

Bernie played coy. 'That ol' floor always gave

them trouble, di'n't it, Malkie? Too low it was, stones too rough, never a decent job of building. But what else c'n you expect when a structure's donkey's ears old?'

Malcolm mined through this non sequitur for meaning. The old buildings in the area were Gloucester Grammar School, the Plantagenet pub, Market Bosworth Hall, the timbered cottages in Rectory Lane, St James Church in—

His gaze sharpened, first on Bernie and then on his document. St James Church in Sutton Cheney, he thought. And he gave the document a closer look.

Which is when he deciphered the first line of it –
I, Richard, by the Grace of God Kyng of England and France and Lord of Ireland – which is when his glance dropped to the hastily scrawled signature, which he also deciphered. *Richard R.*

Holy Jesus God, he thought. What had Bernie got his drunken little hands on?

He knew the importance of staying cool. One indication of his interest and he'd be Bernie's breakfast. So he said, 'Can't tell much in this light, Bernie. Mind if I have a closer look at home?'

But Bernie wasn't about to buy that proposal. He said, 'Can't let it out of m' sight, Malkie. Family legacy, that. Been our goods for donkey's ears, that has, and every one of us swore to keep it safe.'

'How did you ...?' But Malcolm knew better than to ask how Bernie had come to have a letter written by Richard III among his family belongings. Bernie would tell him only what Bernie deemed necessary for Malcolm to know. So he said, 'Let's have a look in the kitchen, then. That all right with you?'

That was just fine with Bernie Perryman. He, after all, wanted his old mate to see what the document was. So they went into the kitchen and sat at the table and Malcolm pored over the thick piece of paper.

The writing was terrible, not the neat hand of the professional scribe who would have attended the King and written his correspondence for him, but the hand of a man in agitated spirits. Malcolm had spent nearly twenty years consuming every scrap of information on Richard Plantagenet, Duke of Gloucester, later Richard III, called the Usurper,

I, Richard

called England's Black Legend, called the Bunch-Backed Toad and virtually every other obloquy imaginable. So he knew how possible it actually was that here in this farmhouse, not two hundred yards from Bosworth Field and little over a mile from St James Church, he was looking at the genuine article. Richard had lived his last night in this vicinity. Richard had fought here. Richard had died here. How unimaginable a circumstance was it that Richard had also written a letter somewhere nearby, in a building where it lay hidden until . . .

Malcolm thought about everything he knew of the area's history. He came up with the fact he needed. 'The floor of St James Church,' he said. 'It was raised two hundred years ago, wasn't it?' And one of the countless ne'er-do-well Perrymans had been there, had probably helped with the work, and had found this letter.

Bernie was watching him, a sly smile tweaking the corners of his mouth. 'Whatcho think it says, Malkie?' he asked. 'Think it might be worth a bob or two?'

Malcolm wanted to strangle him, but instead he studied the priceless document. It wasn't long, just a few lines that, he saw, could have altered the course of history and that would – when finally made public through the historical discourse he instantaneously decided to write – finally redeem the King who for five hundred years had been maligned by an accusation of butchery for which there had never been a shred of proof.

I, Richard, by the Grace of God Kyng of England and France and Lord of Ireland, on thys daye of 21 August 1485 do with thys document hereby enstruct the good fadres of Jervaulx to gyve unto the protection of the beerrer Edward hytherto called Lord Bastarde and hys brother Richard, called Duke of Yrk. Possession of thys document wyll suffyce to identyfie the beerrer as John de la Pole, Earl of Lyncoln, beloved nephew of the Kyng. Wrytten in hast at Suton Chene. Richard R.

Two sentences and a phrase only, but enough to redeem a man's reputation. When the King had died on the field of battle that 22 August 1485, his two young nephews had been alive.

Malcolm looked at Bernie steadily. 'You know what this is, don't you, Bernie?' he asked his old friend.

'Numbskull like me?' Bernie asked. 'Him what couldn't even pass his A levels? How'd I know what that bit of trash is? But what d'you think? Worth something if I flog it?'

'You can't sell this, Bernie.' Malcolm spoke before he thought and much too hastily. Doing so, he inadvertently revealed himself.

Bernie scooped the paper up and manhandled it to his chest. Malcolm winced. God only knew the damage the fool was capable of doing when he was drunk.

'Go easy with that,' Malcolm said. 'It's fragile, Bernie.'

'Like friendship, isn't it?' Bernie said. He tottered from the kitchen.

It would have been shortly after that that Bernie

had moved the document to another location, for Malcolm had never seen it again. But the knowledge of its existence had festered inside him for years. And only with the advent of Betsy had he finally seen a way to make that precious piece of paper his.

And it would be, soon. Just as soon as Betsy got up her nerve to phone him with the terrible news that what she'd thought was a legacy was only – to her utterly unschooled eyes – a bit of old paper suitable for lining the bottom of a parakeet cage.

While awaiting her call, Malcolm put the finishing touches on his *The Truth About Richard and Bosworth Field*, ten years in the writing and wanting only a single, final, and previously unseen historical document to serve as witness to the veracity of his theory about what happened to the two young Princes. The hours that he spent at his typewriter flew by like leaves blown off the trees in Ambion Forest, where once a marsh had protected Richard's south flank from attack by Henry Tudor's mercenary army.

The letter gave credence to Malcolm's surmise

that Richard would have told someone of the boys' whereabouts. Should the battle favour Henry Tudor, the Princes would be in deadly danger, so the night before the battle Richard would finally have had to tell someone his most closely guarded secret: where the two boys were. In that way, if the day went to Tudor, the boys could be fetched from the monastery and spirited out of the country and out of the reach of harm.

John de la Pole, Earl of Lincoln, and beloved nephew to Richard III, would have been the likeliest candidate. He would have been instructed to ride to Yorkshire if the King fell, to safeguard the lives of the boys who would be made legitimate – and hence the biggest threat to the usurper – the moment Henry Tudor married their sister.

John de la Pole would have known the gravity of the boys' danger. But despite the fact that his uncle would have told him where the Princes were hidden, he would never have been given access to them, much less had them handed over to him, without express direction to the monks from the King himself.

The letter would have given him that access. But he'd had to flee to the south instead of to the north. So he couldn't pull it from the stones in St James Church where his uncle had hidden it the night before the battle.

And yet the boys disappeared, never to be heard of again. So who took them?

There could be only one answer to that question: Elizabeth of York, sister to the Princes but also affianced wife of the newly crowned-right-there-on-the-battlefield King.

Hearing the news that her uncle had been defeated, Elizabeth would have seen her options clearly: Queen of England should Henry Tudor retain his throne or sister to a mere youthful King should her brother Edward claim his own legitimacy the moment Henry legitimatized her or suppressed the Act by which she'd been made illegitimate in the first place. Thus, she could be the matriarch of a royal dynasty or a political pawn to be given in marriage to anyone with whom her brother wished to form an alliance.

Sheriff Hutton, her temporary residence, was no great distance from any of the abbeys. Ever her uncle's favourite niece and knowing his bent for things religious, she would have guessed – if Richard hadn't told her directly – where he'd hidden her brothers. And the boys would have gone with her willingly. She was their sister, after all.

'I am Elizabeth of York,' she would have told the abbot in that imperious voice she'd heard used so often by her cunning mother. 'I shall see my brothers alive and well. And instantly.'

How easily it would have been accomplished. The two young Princes seeing their older sister for the first time in who knew how long, running to her, embracing her, eagerly turning to the abbot when she informed them that she'd come for them at last . . . And who was the abbot to deny a Royal Princess – clearly recognized by the boys themselves – her own brothers? Especially in the current situation, with King Richard dead and sitting on the throne a man who'd illustrated his bloodthirstiness by making one of his first acts as King a declaration of treason against all who had fought on the side of Richard at Bosworth Field? Tudor wouldn't look kindly on the abbey that was found to be sheltering

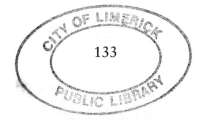

the two boys. God only knew what his revenge would be should he find them.

Thus it made sense for the abbot to deliver Edward the Lord Bastard and his brother Richard the Duke of York into the hands of their sister. And Elizabeth, with her brothers in her possession, handed them over to someone. One of the Stanleys? The duplicitous Earl of Northumberland who went on to serve Henry Tudor in the North? Sir James Tyrell, one-time follower of Richard, who was the recipient of two general pardons from Tudor not a year after he took the throne?

Whoever it was, once the Princes were in his hands, their fates were sealed. And no one wishing to preserve his life afterwards would have thought about levelling an accusation against the wife of a reigning monarch who had already shown his inclination for attainting subjects and confiscating their land.

It was, Malcolm thought, such a brilliant plan on Elizabeth's part. She was her mother's own daughter, after all. She knew the value of placing self-interest above everything else. Besides, she would have told herself that keeping the boys alive would only prolong a struggle for the throne that had been going on for thirty years. She could put an end to the bloodshed by shedding just a little more blood. What woman in her position would have done otherwise?

The fact that it took Betsy more than three months to develop the courage to break the sorrowful news to Malcolm did cause him a twinge of concern now and then. In the time-line he'd long ago written in his mind, she'd have come to him in hysterics not twenty-four hours after discovering that her Legacy was a scribbled-up scrap of dirty paper. She'd have thrown herself into his arms and wept and waited for rescue. To emphasize the dire straits she was in, she'd have brought the paper with her to show him how ill Bernie Perryman had used his loving wife. And he – Malcolm – would have taken the paper from her shaking fingers, would have given it a glance, would have tossed it to the floor and joined in her weeping, mourning the death of their dearly held dreams. For she was ruined financially and he, on a mere paltry salary from Gloucester Grammar, could not offer her the life she deserved. Then, after a vigorous and memorable round of mattress poker, she would leave, the scorned bit of paper still lying on the floor. And the letter would be his. And when his tome was published and the lectures, television interviews, chat shows, and book tours began cluttering up his calendar, he would have no time for a bumpkin housewife who'd been too dim to know what she'd had in her fingers.

That was the plan. Malcolm felt the occasional pinch of worry when it didn't come off quickly and without a hitch. But he told himself that Betsy's reluctance to reveal the truth to him was all part of God's Great Plan. This gave him time to complete his manuscript. And he used the time well.

Since he and Betsy had decided that discretion was in order following Bernie's death, they saw each other only in the corridors of Gloucester Grammar when she returned to work. During this time, Malcolm phoned her nightly for telesex once he realized that he could keep her oiled and proofread the earlier chapters of his opus simultaneously.

Then finally, three months and four days after Bernie's unfortunate demise, Betsy whispered a request to him in the corridor just outside the Headmaster's office. Could he come to the farm for dinner that night? She didn't look as solemn-faced as Malcolm would have liked, considering her impoverished circumstances and the death of her dreams, but he didn't worry much about this. Betsy had already proved herself a stunning actress. She wouldn't want to break down at the school.

Prior to leaving that afternoon, swollen with the recognition that his fantasy was about to be realized, Malcolm handed in his notice to the Headmaster. Samuel Montgomery accepted it with a rather disturbing alacrity which Malcolm didn't much like, and although the Headmaster covered his surprise and delight with a spurious show of regret at losing 'a veritable institution here at GG', Malcolm could see him savouring the triumph of being rid of someone he'd decided was an educational dinosaur. So it gave him more satisfaction than he would have thought possible, knowing how great his own triumph was going to be when he made his mark upon the face of English history.

Malcolm couldn't have been happier as he drove to Windsong Farm that evening. The long winter of his discontent had segued into a beautiful spring, and he was minutes away from being able to right a five-hundred-year-old wrong at the same time as he carved a place for himself in the pantheon of the Historical Greats. God is good, he thought as he made the turn into the farm's long driveway. It was unfortunate that Bernie Perryman had had to die, but as his death was in the interests of historical redemption, it would have to be said that the end richly justified the means.

As he got out of the car, Betsy opened the farmhouse door. Malcolm blinked at her, puzzled at her manner of dress. It took him a moment to digest the fact that she was wearing a full-length fur coat. Silver mink by the look of it, or possibly ermine. It wasn't the wisest get-up to don in these days of animal rights activists, but Betsy had never been a woman to think very far beyond her own desires.

I, Richard

Before Malcolm had a moment to wonder how Betsy had managed to finance the purchase of a fur coat, she had thrown it open and was standing in the doorway, naked to her toes.

'Darling!' she cried. 'We're rich, rich, rich. And you'll never guess what I sold to make us so!'

The Surprise of His Life

The Surprise of His Life

·

When Douglas Armstrong had his first consultation with Thistle McCloud, he had no intention of murdering his wife. His mind, in fact, didn't turn to murder until two weeks after consultation number four.

Douglas watched closely as Thistle prepared herself for a revelation from another dimension. She held his wedding band in the palm of her left hand. She closed her fingers around it. She hovered her right hand over the fist she'd made. She hummed five notes that sounded suspiciously like the beginning of 'I Love You Truly'. Gradually, her eyes rolled back, up, and out of view beneath her yellow-shaded lids, leaving him with the disconcerting sight of a thirty-something female in a straw boater, white shirt and polka-dotted tie, looking as if she were one quarter of a barber-shop quartet in desperate hope of finding her partners.

When he'd first seen Thistle, Douglas had appraised her attire – which in subsequent visits had not altered in any appreciable fashion – as the insidious get-up of a charlatan who wished to focus her clients' attention on her personal appearance rather than on whatever machinations she would be going through to delve into their pasts, their presents, their futures, and – most importantly – their wallets. But he'd come to realize that Thistle's odd get-up had nothing to do with distracting anyone. The first time she held his old Rolex watch and began speaking in a low, intense voice about the prodigal son, about his endless departures and equally endless returns, about his ageing parents who welcomed him always with open arms and open hearts, and about his brother who watched all this with a false fixed smile and a silent shout of, What about me? Do I mean nothing?, he had a feeling that Thistle was exactly what she purported to be: a psychic.

The Surprise of His Life

He'd first come to her store-front operation because he'd had forty minutes to kill prior to his yearly prostate exam. He dreaded the exam and the teeth-grating embarrassment of having to answer his doctor's jovial, rib-poking, 'Everything up and about as it should be?' with the truth, which was that Newton's law of gravity had begun asserting itself lately into his dearest appendage. And since he was six weeks short of his fifty-fifth birthday, and since every disaster in his life had occurred in a year that was a multiple of five, if there was a chance of knowing what the gods had in store for him and his prostate, he wanted to be able to do something to head off the chaos.

These things had all been in his mind as he spun along Pacific Coast Highway in the dim gold light of a late December afternoon. On a drearily commercialized section of the road – given largely to pizza parlours and boogie-board shops – he had seen the small blue building that he'd passed a thousand times before and read *Psychic Consultations* on its hand-painted sign. He'd glanced at his gas gauge for an excuse to stop and while he pumped super unleaded into the tank of his Mercedes across the street from that small blue building, he made his decision. What the hell, he'd thought. There were worse ways to kill forty minutes.

So he'd had his first session with Thistle McCloud, who was anything but what he'd expected of a psychic since she used no crystal ball, no Tarot cards, nothing at all but a piece of his jewellery. In his first three visits, it had always been the Rolex watch from which she'd received her psychic emanations. But today she'd placed the watch to one side, declared it diluted of power, and set her fog-coloured eyes on his wedding ring. She'd touched her finger to it, and said, 'I'll use that, I think, if you want something further from your history and closer to your heart.'

He'd given her the ring precisely because of those last two phrases: *further from your history and closer to your heart*. They told him how very well she knew that the prodigal son business rose from his past while his deepest concerns were about his future.

With the ring now in her closed fist and with her eyes rolled upward, Thistle stopped the five-note humming, breathed deeply six times, and opened her eyes. She observed him with a melancholia that made his stomach feel hollow.

'What?' Douglas asked.

'You need to prepare yourself for a shock,' she said. 'It's something unexpected. It comes out of nowhere and because of it, the essence of your life will be changed forever. And soon. I feel it coming very soon.'

Jesus, he thought. It was just what he needed to hear three weeks after having had an indifferent index finger shoved up his ass to see what was the cause of his limp dick syndrome. The doctor had said it wasn't cancer, but he hadn't ruled out half a dozen other possibilities. Douglas wondered which one of them Thistle had tuned her psychic antennae into.

Thistle opened her hand, and they both looked at his wedding ring, faintly sheened by her sweat. 'It's an external shock,' she clarified. 'The source of upheaval in your life isn't from within. The shock comes from outside and rattles you to your core.'

'Are you sure about that?' Douglas asked her.

'As sure as I can be, considering the armour you

wear.' Thistle returned his ring to him, her cool fingers grazing his wrist. She said, 'Your name isn't David, is it? It never was David. It never will be David. But the *D*, I feel, is correct. Am I right?'

He reached into his back pocket and brought out his wallet. Careful to shield his driver's licence from her, he clipped a fifty dollar bill between his thumb and index finger. He folded it once and handed it over.

'Donald,' she said. 'No. That isn't it either. Darrell perhaps. Dennis. I sense two syllables.'

'Names aren't important in your line of work, are they?' Douglas asked.

'No. But the truth is always important. Someday, Not-David, you're going to have to learn to trust people with the truth. Trust is the key. Trust is essential.'

'Trust', he told her, 'is what gets people screwed.'

Outside, he walked across the coast highway to the cramped side street that paralleled the ocean. Here he always parked his car when he visited Thistle. With its vanity licence plate DRIL4IT virtually announcing who owned the Mercedes, Douglas had early on decided that it wouldn't encourage new investors if anyone put out the word that the president of South Coast Oil had begun seeing a psychic regularly. Risky investments were one thing. Placing money with a man who could be accused of using parapsychology rather than geology to find oil deposits was another. He wasn't doing that, of course. Business never came up in his sessions with Thistle. But try telling that to the Board of Directors. Try telling that to anyone.

He unarmed the car and slid inside. He headed south, in the direction of his office. As far as anyone at South Coast Oil knew, he'd spent his lunch hour with his wife having a romantic winter's picnic on the bluffs in Corona del Mar. The cellular phone will be turned off for an hour, he'd informed his secretary. Don't try to phone and don't bother us, please. This is time for Donna and me. She deserves it. I need it. Are we clear on the subject?

Any mention of Donna always did the trick when it came to keeping South Coast Oil off his back for a few hours. She was warmly liked by everyone in the company. She was warmly liked by everyone period. Sometimes, he reflected, she was too warmly liked. Especially by men.

You need to prepare for a shock.

Did he? Douglas considered the question in relation to his wife.

When he pointed out men's affinity for her, Donna always acted surprised. She told him that men merely recognized in her a woman who'd grown up in a household of brothers. But what Douglas saw in men's eyes when they looked at his wife had nothing to do with fraternal affection. It had to do with getting her naked, getting down and dirty, and getting laid.

Getting laid was behind every man-woman interaction on the planet. Douglas knew this well. So while his recent failures to get it up and get it on with Donna frustrated him, his real fear was that her patience with him was trickling away. Once it was gone, she'd start looking around. That was natural. And once she started looking, she was going to find or be found herself.

The shock comes from outside and rattles you to your core.

Shit, Douglas thought. If chaos was about to steamroller into his life as he approached his fifty-fifth birthday – that rotten bad luck integer – Douglas had to admit that his wife Donna would probably be sitting at the wheel. She was thirty-five, four years in place as wife number three, and while she acted content, he'd been around women long enough to know that still waters did more than simply run deep. They hid rocks that could sink a boat in seconds if a sailor didn't keep his wits about him. And love made people lose their wits, didn't it? Didn't love make people go a little bit nuts?

Of course, *he* wasn't nuts. He had his wits about him. But being in love with a woman twenty years his junior, a woman whose scent caught the nose of every male within sixty yards of her, a woman whose physical appetites he was failing to satisfy on a nightly basis . . . and had been failing to satisfy for weeks . . . a woman like that . . .

'Get a grip,' Douglas told himself brusquely. 'This psychic stuff is bullshit, right? Right.' But still he thought of the coming shock, the upset to his life, and its source: external. Not his prostate, not his dick, not an organ in his body. But another human being. 'Shit,' he said.

He guided the car up the incline that led to Jamboree Boulevard, six lanes of concrete that rolled between stunted liquidambar trees through some of the most expensive real estate in Orange County. It took him to the bronzed glass tower that housed his pride: South Coast Oil.

Once inside the building, he navigated his way through an unexpected encounter with two of SCO's engineers, through a brief conversation with a geologist who simultaneously waved an ordnance survey map and a report from the EPA, and through a hallway conference with the head of the accounting department. His secretary handed him a fistful of messages when he finally managed to reach his office. She said, 'Nice picnic? The weather's unbelievable, isn't it?' followed by 'Everything all right, Mr Armstrong?' when he didn't reply.

He said, 'Yes. What? Fine,' and looked through the messages. He found that the names meant nothing to him. Absolutely nothing.

He walked to the window behind his desk and looked at the view through its enormous pane of tinted glass. Below him, Orange County's airport sent jet after jet hurtling into the air at an angle so acute that it defied both reason and aerodynamics, although it did protect the delicate auditory sensibilities of the millionaires who lived in the flight path below. Douglas watched these planes without really seeing them. He knew he had to answer his telephone messages, but all he could think about were Thistle's words: *an external shock*.

What could be more external than Donna?

She wore Obsession. She put it behind her ears and beneath her breasts. Whenever she passed through a room, she left the scent of herself behind.

Her dark hair gleamed when the sunlight hit it. She wore it short and simply cut, parted on the left and smoothly falling just to her ears.

Her legs were long. When she walked, her stride was full and sure. And when she walked with him – at his side, with her hand through his arm and her head held back – he knew that she caught the attention of everyone. He knew that together they

153

were the envy of all of their friends and of strangers as well.

He could see this reflected in the faces of people they passed when he and Donna were together. At the ballet, at the theatre, at concerts, in restaurants, glances gravitated to Douglas Armstrong and his wife. In women's expressions, he could read the wish to be young like Donna, to be smooth-skinned again, to be vibrant once more, to be fecund and ready. In men's expression, he could read desire.

It had always been a pleasure to see how others reacted to the sight of his wife. But now he saw how dangerous her allure really was and how it threatened to destroy his peace.

A shock, Thistle had said. *Prepare for a shock. Prepare for a shock that will change your world.*

That evening, Douglas heard the water running as soon as he entered the house: fifty-two hundred square feet of limestone floors, vaulted ceilings, and picture windows on a hillside that offered an ocean view to the west and the lights of Orange County to the east. The house had cost him a fortune, but that had been all right with him. Money meant nothing. He'd bought the place for Donna. But if he'd had doubts about his wife before – born of his own per-formance anxiety, growing to adulthood through his consultation with Thistle – when Douglas heard that water running, he began to see the truth. Because Donna was in the shower.

He watched her silhouette behind the blocks of translucent glass that defined the shower's wall. She was washing her hair. She hadn't noticed him yet, and he watched her for a moment, his gaze travelling over her uplifted breasts, her hips, her long legs. She usually bathed – languorous bubble baths in the raised oval tub that looked out on the lights of the city of Irvine. Taking a shower suggested a more energetic and earnest effort to cleanse herself. And washing her hair suggested . . . Well, it was perfectly clear what that suggested. Scents got caught up in the hair: cigarette smoke, sautéing garlic, fish from a fishing boat, or semen and sex. Those last two were the betraying scents. Obviously, she would have to wash her hair.

Her discarded clothes lay on the floor. With a hasty

glance at the shower, Douglas fingered through them and found her lacy underwear. He knew women. He knew his wife. If she'd actually been with a man that afternoon, her body's leaking juices would have made the panties' crotch stiff when they dried, and he would be able to smell the afterscent of intercourse on them. They would give him proof. He lifted them to his face.

'Doug! What on earth are you doing?'

Douglas dropped the panties, cheeks hot and neck sweating. Donna was peering at him from the shower's opening, her hair lathered with soap that streaked down her left cheek. She brushed it away.

'What are *you* doing?' he asked her. Three marriages and two divorces had taught him that a fast offensive manoeuvre threw the opponent off balance. It worked.

She popped back into the water – clever of her, so he couldn't see her face – and said, 'It's pretty obvious. I'm taking a shower. God, what a day.'

He moved to watch her through the shower's opening. There was no door, just a partition in the glass-blocked wall. He could study her body and look for the telltale signs of the kind of rough love-making he knew that she liked. And she wouldn't know that he was even looking since her head was beneath the shower as she rinsed off her hair.

'Steve phoned in sick today,' she said, 'so I had to do everything at the kennels myself.' She raised chocolate labradors. He had met her that way, seeking a dog for his youngest son. Through a reference from a veterinarian, he had discovered her kennels in Midway City – less than one square mile of feed-stores, other kennels, and dilapidated post-war stucco and shake roofs posing as suburban housing. It was an odd place for a girl from the pricey side of Corona del Mar to end up professionally, but that was what he liked about Donna. She wasn't true to type, she wasn't a beach bunny, she wasn't a typical southern California girl. Or at least that's what he had thought.

'The worst was cleaning the dog runs,' she said. 'I didn't mind the grooming – I never mind that – but I hate doing the runs. I completely reeked of dog poop when I got home.' She shut off the shower and reached for her towels, wrapping her head in one and her body in the other. She stepped out of the stall with a smile and said, 'Isn't it weird how some smells cling to your body and your hair while others don't?'

She kissed him hello and scooped up her clothes. She tossed them down the laundry chute. No doubt she was thinking, Out of sight, out of mind. She was clever that way.

'That's the third time Steve's phoned in sick in two weeks.' She headed for the bedroom, drying off as she went. She dropped the towel with her usual absence of self-consciousness and began dressing, pulling on wispy underwear, black leggings, a silver tunic. 'If this keeps up, I'm going to let him go. I need someone consistent, someone reliable. If he's not going to be able to hold up his end . . .' She frowned at Douglas, her face perplexed. 'What's wrong, Doug? You're looking at me so funny. Is something wrong?'

'Wrong? No.' But he thought, That looks like a love bite on her neck. And he crossed to her for a better look. He cupped her face for a kiss and tilted her head. The shadow of the towel that was wrapped round her head dissipated, leaving her skin unmarred. Well, what of it? He thought. She wouldn't be so stupid as to let some heavy breather suck bruises into her flesh, no matter how turned on he had her. She wasn't that dumb. Not his Donna.

But she also wasn't as smart as her husband.

At 5:45, he went to the personnel department. It was a better choice than the Yellow Pages because at least he knew that whoever had been doing the background checks on incoming employees at South Coast Oil was simultaneously competent and discreet. No one had ever complained about some two-bit gumshoe nosing into his background.

The department was deserted, as he'd hoped. The computer screens at every desk were set to shifting images that preserved them: a field of swimming fish, bouncing balls, and popping bubbles. The director's office at the far side of the department was unlit and locked, but a master key in the hand of the company president solved that problem. Douglas went inside and flipped on the lights.

He found the name he was looking for among

the dog-eared cards of the director's Rolodex, a curious anachronism in an otherwise computer-age office. *Cowley and Son, Inquiries*, he read in faded typescript. This was accompanied by a telephone number and by an address on Balboa Peninsula.

Douglas studied both for the space of two minutes. Was it better to know or to live in ignorant bliss? But he wasn't living in bliss, was he? And he hadn't been living in bliss from the moment he'd failed to perform as a man was meant to. So it was better to know. Some things in life one had to know, whatever the consequences.

He picked up the phone.

Douglas always went out for lunch – unless a conference was scheduled with his geologists or the engineers – so no one raised a hair of an eyebrow when he left South Coast Oil before noon the following day. He used Jamboree once again to get to the coast highway, but this time instead of heading north toward Newport where Thistle made her prognostications, he drove directly across the highway and down the incline where a modestly arched bridge spanned an oily stretch of Newport Harbour that divided the mainland from an amoeba-shaped portion of land that was Balboa Island.

In summer the island was infested with tourists, who bottled up the streets with their cars and rode their bicycles in races on the sidewalk around the island's perimeter. No local in his right mind ventured onto Balboa Island during the summer without good reason, unless he lived there. But in winter, the place was virtually deserted. It took less than five minutes to snake through the narrow streets to the island's north end where the ferry waited to take cars and pedestrians on the eye-blink voyage across to the peninsula.

There, a stripe-topped carousel and a Ferris wheel spun like two opposing gears of an enormous clock, defining an area called the Fun Zone, which had long been the summertime bane of the local police. Today, however, no bands of juveniles roved with cans of spray paint at the ready. The only inhabitants of the Fun Zone were a paraplegic in a wheelchair and his bike-riding companion.

Douglas passed them as he drove off the ferry.

161

They were intent upon their conversation. The Ferris wheel and carousel did not exist for them. Nor did Douglas and his blue Mercedes, which was just as well. He didn't particularly want to be seen.

He parked just off the beach, in a lot where fifteen minutes cost a quarter. He pumped in four. He armed the car and headed west toward Main Street, a tree-shaded lane some sixty yards long that began at a *faux* New England restaurant overlooking Newport Harbour and ended at Balboa Pier, which stretched out into the Pacific Ocean, grey-green today and unsettled by roiling waves from a winter Alaskan storm.

Number 107-B Main was what he was looking for, and he found it easily. Just east of an alley, 107 was a two-storey structure whose bottom floor was taken up by a time-warped hair salon called JJ's – heavily devoted to macramé, potted plants, and posters of Janis Joplin – and whose upper floor was divided into offices that were reached by a structurally questionable stairway at the north end of the building. 107-B was the first door upstairs – JJ's Natural Haircutting appeared to be 107-A

– but when Douglas turned the discoloured brass knob below the equally discoloured brass nameplate announcing the business as *Cowley and Son, Inquiries*, he found the door locked.

He frowned and looked at his Rolex. His appointment was for 12:15. It was currently 12:10. So where was Cowley? Where was his son?

He returned to the stairway, ready to head to his car and his cellular phone, ready to track down Cowley and give him hell for setting up an appointment and failing to be there to keep it. But he was three steps down when he saw a khaki clad man coming his way, sucking up an Orange Julius with the enthusiasm of a twelve-year-old. His thinning grey hair and sun-lined face marked him at least five decades older than twelve, however. And his limping gait – in combination with his clothes – suggested old war wounds.

'You Cowley?' Douglas called from the stairs.

The man waved his Orange Julius in reply. 'You Armstrong?' he asked.

'Right,' Douglas said. 'Listen, I don't have a lot of time.'

'None of us do, son,' Cowley said, and he hoisted himself up the stairway. He nodded in a friendly fashion, pulled hard at the Orange Julius straw, and passed Douglas in a gust of aftershave that he hadn't smelled for a good twenty years. Canoe. Jesus. Did they still sell that?

Cowley swung the door open and cocked his head to indicate that Douglas was to enter. The office comprised two rooms: one was a sparsely furnished waiting area through which they passed; the other was obviously Cowley's demesne. Its centrepiece was an olive green steel desk. Filing cabinets and bookshelves of the same issue matched it.

The investigator went to an old oak office chair behind the desk, but he didn't sit. Instead, he opened one of the side drawers and, just when Douglas was expecting him to pull out a fifth of bourbon, he dug out a bottle of yellow pills instead. He shook six of them into his palm and knocked them back with a long swig of Orange Julius. He sank into his chair and gripped its arms.

'Arthritis,' he said. 'I'm killing it with evening

primrose oil. Give me a minute, okay? You want a couple?'

'No.' Douglas glanced at his watch to make certain Cowley knew that his time was precious. Then he strolled to the steel bookshelves.

He was expecting to see munitions manuals, penal codes, and surveillance texts, something to assure the prospective clients that they'd come to the right place with their troubles. But what he found was poetry, volume after volume neatly arranged in alphabetical order by author, from Matthew Arnold to William Butler Yeats. He wasn't sure what to think.

The occasional space left at the end of a bookshelf was taken up by photographs. They were clumsily framed, snapshots mostly. They depicted grinning small children, a grey-haired grandma type, several young adults. Among them, encased in Plexiglass, was a military Purple Heart. Douglas picked this up. He'd never seen one, but he was pleased to know that his guess about the source of Cowley's limp had been correct.

'You saw action,' he said.

'My butt saw action,' Cowley replied. Douglas

looked his way, so the investigator continued. 'I took it in the ass. Shit happens, right?' He moved his hands from their grip on the arms of his chair. He folded them over his stomach. Like Douglas's own, it could have been flatter. Indeed, the two men shared a similar build: stocky, quickly given to weight if they didn't exercise, too tall to be called short and too short to be called tall. 'What can I do for you, Mr Armstrong?'

'My wife,' Douglas said.

'Your wife?'

'She may be . . .' Now that it was time to articulate the problem, Douglas wasn't sure that he could. So he said, 'Who's the son?'

'What?'

'It says Cowley and Son, but there's only one desk. Who's the son?'

Cowley reached for his Orange Julius and took a pull on its straw. 'He died,' he said. 'Drunk driver got him on Ortega Highway.'

'Sorry.'

'Like I said. Shit happens. What shit's happened to you?'

Douglas returned the Purple Heart to its place. He caught sight of the greying grandma in one of the pictures and said, 'This your wife?'

'Forty years my wife. Name's Maureen.'

'I'm on my third. How'd you manage forty years with one woman?'

'She has a sense of humour.' Cowley slid open the middle drawer of his desk and took out a legal pad and the stub of a pencil. He wrote *Armstrong* at the top in block letters and underlined it. He said, 'About your wife . . .'

'I think she's having an affair. I want to know if I'm right. I want to know who it is.'

Cowley carefully set down his pencil. He observed Douglas for a moment. Outside, a gull gave a raucous cry from one of the rooftops. 'What makes you think she's seeing someone?'

'Am I supposed to give you proof before you'll take the case. I thought that's why I was hiring you. To give *me* proof.'

'You wouldn't be here if you didn't have suspicions. What are they?'

Douglas raked through his memory. He wasn't

about to tell Cowley about trying to smell up Donna's underwear, so he took a moment to examine her behaviour over the last few weeks. And when he did so, the additional evidence was there. Jesus, how the hell had he missed it? She'd changed her hair; she'd bought new underwear – that black lacy Victoria's Secret stuff; she'd been on the phone twice when he'd come home and as soon as he walked into the room, she'd hung up hastily; there were at least two long absences with insufficient excuse for them; there were six or seven engagements that she'd said were with friends.

Cowley nodded thoughtfully when Douglas listed his suspicions. Then he said, 'Have you given her a reason to cheat on you?'

'A reason? What is this? I'm the guilty party?'

'Women don't usually stray without there being a man behind them, giving them a reason.' Cowley examined him from beneath unclipped eyebrows. One of his eyes, Douglas saw, was beginning to form a cataract. Jeez, the guy was ancient. A real antique.

'No reason,' Douglas said. 'I don't cheat on her. I don't even want to.'

'She's young, though. And a man your age . . .' Cowley shrugged. 'Shit happens to us old guys. Young things don't always have the patience to understand.'

Douglas wanted to point out that Cowley was at least ten years his senior, if not more. He also wanted to take himself from membership in the club of *us old guys*. But the detective was watching him compassionately, so instead of arguing, Douglas told the truth.

Cowley reached for his Orange Julius and drained the cup. He tossed it in the trash. 'Women have needs,' he said, and he moved his hand from his crotch to his chest, adding, 'A wise man doesn't confuse what goes on here –' the crotch – 'with what goes on here' – the chest.

'So maybe I'm not wise. Are you going to help me out or not?'

'You sure you want help?'

'I want to know the truth. I can live with that. What I can't live with is not knowing. I just need to know what I'm dealing with here.'

Cowley looked as if he was taking a reading of Douglas's level of veracity. He finally appeared to make a decision, but one he apparently didn't like because he shook his head, picked up his pencil, and said, 'Give me some background, then. If she's got someone on the side, who're our possibilities?'

Douglas had already thought about this. There was Mike, the pool-man who visited once a week. There was Steve, who worked with Donna at her kennels in Midway City. There was Jeff, her personal trainer. There were also the postman, the Fed Ex man, the UPS driver, and Donna's too-youthful gynaecologist.

'I take it you're accepting the case?' Douglas said to Cowley. He pulled out his wallet from which he extracted a wad of bills. 'You'll be wanting a retainer.'

'I don't need cash, Mr Armstrong.'

'All the same . . .' All the same, Douglas had no intention of leaving a paper trail via a cheque. 'How much time do you need?' he asked.

'Give it a few days. If she's seeing someone, he'll surface eventually. They always do.' Cowley sounded despondent.

'Your wife cheat on you?' Douglas asked shrewdly.

'If she did, I probably deserved it.'

That was Cowley's attitude, but it was one that Douglas didn't share. He didn't deserve to be cheated on. Nobody did. And when he found out who was doing the job on his wife ... Well, they would see a kind of justice that Attila the Hun had been incapable of extracting.

His resolve was strengthened in the bedroom that evening when his hello kiss to his wife was interrupted by the telephone. Donna pulled away from him quickly and went to answer it. She gave Douglas a smile – as if recognizing what her haste revealed – and shook back her hair as sexily as possible, running slim fingers through her hair as she picked up the receiver.

Douglas listened to her side of the conversation while he changed his clothes. He heard her voice brighten as she said, 'Yes, yes. Hello ... No ... Doug just got home and we were talking about the day ...'

So her caller knew he was in the room. Douglas could imagine what the bastard was saying, whoever he was: *'So you can't talk?'*

To which Donna, on cue, answered, 'Nope. Not at all.'

'Shall I call later?'

'Gosh, that would be nice.'

'Today was what was nice, baby. I love to fuck you.'

'Really? Outrageous. I'll have to check it out.'

'I want to check you out, babe. Are you wet for me?'

'I sure am. Listen, we'll connect later on, okay? I need to get dinner started.'

'Just as long as you remember today. It was the best. You're the best.'

'Right. Bye.' She hung up and came to him. She put her arms round his waist. She said, 'Got rid of her. Nancy Talbert. God. Nothing's more important in her life than a shoe sale at Neiman-Marcus. Spare me. Please.' She snuggled up to him. He couldn't see her face, just the back of her head where it reflected in the mirror.

'Nancy Talbert?' he said. 'I don't think I know her.'

'Sure you do, honey.' She pressed her hips against him. He felt the hopeful but useless heat in his groin. 'She's in Soroptimists with me. You met her last month after the ballet. Hmm. You feel nice. Gosh, I like it when you hold me, Doug. Should I start dinner or d'you want to mess around?'

Another clever move on her part: he wouldn't think she was cheating if she still wanted it from him. No matter that he couldn't give it to her. She was hanging in there with him and this moment proved it. Or so she thought.

'Love to,' he said and smacked her on the butt. 'But let's eat first. And after, right there on the dining room table . . .' He managed what he hoped was a lewd enough wink. 'Just you wait, kiddo.'

She laughed and released him and went off to the kitchen. He walked to the bed where he sat disconsolately. The charade was torture. He had to know the truth.

He didn't hear from Cowley and Son, Inquiries,

for two agonizing weeks during which he suffered through three more coy telephone conversations between Donna and her lover, four more phoney excuses to cover unscheduled absences from home, and two more midday showers sloughed off to Steve's absence from the kennels again. By the time he finally made contact with Cowley, Douglas's nerves were shot.

Cowley had news to report. He said he'd hand it over as soon as they could meet. 'How's lunch?' Cowley asked. 'We could do Tail of the Whale over here.'

No lunch, Douglas told him. He wouldn't be able to eat anyway. He would meet Cowley at his office at 12:45.

'Make it the pier, then,' Cowley said. 'I'll catch a burger at Ruby's and we can talk after. You know Ruby's? The end of the pier?'

Who didn't know Ruby's? A fifties' coffee shop, it sat at the end of Balboa Pier, and he found Cowley there as promised at 12:45, polishing off a bacon cheeseburger and fries, with a manila envelope sitting next to his strawberry milk-shake.

Cowley wore the same khakis he'd had on the day they'd met. He'd added a panama hat to his ensemble. He touched his index finger to the hat's brim as Douglas approached him. His cheeks were bulging with burger and fries.

Douglas slid into the booth opposite Cowley and reached for the envelope. Cowley's hand slapped down on it. 'Not yet,' he said.

'I've got to know.'

Cowley slid the envelope off the table and onto the vinyl seat next to himself. He twirled the straw in his milk-shake and observed Douglas through opaque eyes that seemed to reflect the sunlight outside. 'Pictures,' he said. 'That's all I've got for you. Pictures aren't the truth. You got that?'

'Okay. Pictures.'

'I don't know what I'm shooting. I just tail the woman and I shoot what I see. What I see may not mean shit. You understand?'

'Just show me the pictures.'

'Outside.'

Cowley tossed a five and three ones onto the table, called, 'Catch you later, Susie', to the waitress and led the way. He walked to the railing where he looked out over the water. A whale-watching boat was bobbing some quarter mile off shore. It was too early in the year to catch sight of a pod migrating to Alaska, but the tourists on board probably wouldn't know that. Their binoculars winked in the light.

When Douglas joined the investigator, Cowley said, 'You got to know that she doesn't act like a woman guilty of anything. She just seems to be doing her thing. She met a few men – I won't mislead you – but I couldn't catch her doing anything cheesy.'

'Give me the pictures.'

Cowley gave him a sharp look instead. Douglas knew his voice was betraying him. 'I say we tail her for another two-three weeks,' Cowley said. 'What I've got here isn't much to go on.' He opened the envelope. He stood so that Douglas only saw the back of the pictures. He chose to hand them over in sets.

The first set was taken in Midway City not far from the kennels, at the feed and grain store where Donna bought food for the dogs. In these, she was loading fifty pound food sacks into the back of her

Toyota pick-up. She was being assisted by a Calvin Klein type in tight jeans and a T-shirt. They were laughing together, and in one of the pictures Donna had perched her sunglasses on top of her head, the better to look at her companion directly.

She appeared to be flirting, but she was a young, pretty woman and flirting was normal. This seemed okay. She could have looked less happy to be chatting with the stud, but she was a business woman and she was conducting business. Douglas could deal with that.

The second set was of Donna in the Newport gym where she worked with a personal trainer twice a week. Her trainer was one of those sculpted bodies with a head of hair on which every strand looked as if it had been seen to professionally on a daily basis. In the pictures, Donna was dressed to work out – nothing Douglas had not seen before – but for the first time he noted how carefully she assembled her work-out clothes. From the leggings to the leotard to the headband she wore, everything enhanced her. The trainer appeared to recognize this because he squatted before her as she did her vertical butterflies.

Her legs were spread and there was no doubt what he was concentrating on. This looked more serious.

He was about to ask Cowley to start tailing the trainer, when the investigator said, 'No body contact between them other than what you'd expect,' and handed him the last set of pictures, saying, 'These're the only ones that look a little shaky to me, but they may mean nothing. You know this guy?'

Douglas stared, with *know this guy, know this guy* ringing in his skull. Unlike the other pictures in which Donna and her companion-of-the-moment were in one location, these showed Donna at a view table in an ocean-front restaurant, Donna on the Balboa ferry, Donna walking along a dock in Newport. In each of these pictures, she was with a man, the same man. In each of these pictures there was body contact. It was nothing extreme because they were out in public. But it was the kind of body contact that betrayed: an arm around her shoulders, a kiss on her cheek, a full body hug that said, Feel me up, baby, cause I ain't limp like him.

Douglas felt that his world was spinning, but he

managed a wry grin. He said, 'Oh hell. Now I feel like a class-A fool.'

'Why's that?' Cowley asked.

'This guy?' Douglas indicated the athletic-looking man in the picture with Donna. 'Jesus. This is her brother.'

'You're kidding.'

'Nope. He's a walk-on coach at Newport Harbour High. His name is Mike. He's a free spirit type.' Douglas gripped the railing with one hand and shook his head with what he hoped looked like chagrin. 'Is this all you've got?'

'That's it. I can tail her for a while longer and see—'

'Nah. Forget it. Jesus. I sure feel dumb.' Douglas ripped the photographs into confetti. He tossed this into the water where it formed a mantle that was quickly shredded by the waves that arced against the pier's pilings. 'What do I owe you, Mr Cowley?' he asked. 'What's this dumb ass got to pay for not trusting the finest woman on earth?'

He took Cowley to Dillman's on the corner of Main

and Balboa Boulevard, and they sat at the snake-like bar with the locals, where they knocked back a couple of brews apiece. Douglas worked on his affability act, playing the abashed husband who suddenly realizes what a dickhead he's been. He took all of Donna's actions over the past weeks and reinterpreted them for Cowley. The unexplained absences became the foundation for a treat she was planning for him: the purchase of a new car, perhaps; a trip to Europe; the refurbishing of his boat. The secretive telephone calls became messages from his children who were in the know. The new underwear metamorphosed into a display of her wish to make herself desirable for him, to work him out of his temporary impotence by giving him a renewed interest in her body. He felt like a total idiot, he told Cowley. Could they burn the damn negatives together?

They made a ceremony of it, torching the negatives of the damning pictures in the alley behind JJ's Natural Haircutting. Afterwards, Douglas drove in a daze to Newport Harbour High School. He sat numbly across the street from it. He waited two hours. Finally, he saw his youngest brother arrive for the afternoon's coaching session, a basketball tucked under his arm and an athletic bag in his hand.

Michael, he thought. Returned from Greece this time, but always the prodigal son. Before Greece, it was a year with Greenpeace on the *Rainbow Warrior*. Before that, it was an expedition up the Amazon. And before that, it was marching against apartheid in South Africa. He had a resumé that would be the envy of any pre-pubescent kid out for a good time. He was Mr Adventure, Mr Irresponsibility, and Mr Charm. He was Mr Good Intentions without any follow-through. When a promise was due to be kept, he was out of sight, out of mind, and out of the country. But everyone loved the son of a bitch. He was forty years old, the baby of the Armstrong brothers, and he always got precisely what he wanted.

He wanted Donna now, the miserable bastard. No matter that she was his brother's wife. That made having her just so much more fun.

Douglas felt ill. His guts rolled around like marbles in a bucket. Sweat broke out in patches on his body. He couldn't go back to work like this. He reached for the phone and called his office.

He was sick, he told his secretary. Must have been something he ate for lunch. He was heading home. She could catch him there if anything came up.

In the house, he wandered from room to room. Donna wasn't home – wouldn't be home for hours – so he had plenty of time to consider what to do. His mind reproduced for him the pictures that Cowley had taken of Michael and Donna. His intellect deduced where they had been and what they'd been doing prior to those pictures being taken.

He went to his study. There, in a glass curio cabinet, his collection of ivory erotica mocked him. Miniature Asians posed in a variety of sexual postures, having themselves a roaring good time. He could see Michael and Donna's features superimposed on the creamy faces of the figurines. They took their pleasure at his expense. They justified their pleasure by using his failure. No limp dick here, Michael's voice taunted. What's the matter, big brother? Can't hang onto your wife?

Douglas felt shattered. He told himself that he

could have handled her doing anything else, he could have handled seeing her with anyone else. But not Michael, who had trailed him through life, making his mark in every area where Douglas himself had previously failed. In high school it had been in athletics and student government. In college it had been in the world of fraternities. As an adult it had been in embracing adventure rather than in tackling the grind of business. And now, it was in proving to Donna what real manhood was all about.

Douglas could see them together as easily as he could see his pieces of erotica intertwined. Their bodies joined, their heads thrown back, their hands clasped, their hips grinding and grinding against each other. God, he thought. The pictures in his mind would drive him mad. He felt like killing.

The telephone company gave him the proof he required. He asked for a print-out of the calls that had been made from his home. And when he received it, there was Michael's number. Not once or twice, but repeatedly. All of the calls had been made when he – Douglas – wasn't at home.

183

It was clever of Donna to use the nights when she knew Douglas would be doing his volunteer stint at the Newport suicide hotline. She knew he never missed his Wednesday evening shift, so important was it to him to have the hotline among his community commitments. She knew he was building a political profile to get himself elected to the city council, and the hotline was part of the picture of himself that he wished to paint: Douglas Armstrong, husband, father, oilman, and compassionate listener to the emotionally distressed. He needed something to put into the balance of his environmental lapses. The hotline allowed him to say that while he may have spilled oil on a few lousy pelicans – not to mention some miserable otters – he would never let a human life hang there in jeopardy.

Donna had known he'd never skip even a part of his evening shift, so she'd waited till then to make her calls to Michael. There they were on the print-out, every one of them made between 6:00 and 9:00 on a Wednesday night.

Okay, the bitch liked Wednesday night so well. Wednesday night would be the night that he killed her.

        *   *   *

He could hardly bear to be around her once he had the proof of her betrayal. She knew something was wrong between them because he didn't want to touch her any longer. Their thrice-weekly attempted couplings – as disastrous as they'd been – fast became a thing of the past. Still, she carried on as if nothing and no one had come between them, sashaying through the bedroom in her Victoria's Secret selection-of-the-night, trying to entice him into making a fool of himself so she could share the laughter with his brother Michael.

No way, baby, Douglas thought. You'll be sorry you made a fool out of me.

When she finally cuddled next to him in bed and murmured, 'Doug, is something wrong? You want to talk? You okay?' it was all he could do not to shove her from him. He wasn't okay. He would never be okay again. But at least he'd be able to salvage a measure of his self-respect by giving the little bitch her due.

It was easy enough to plan once he decided on the very next Wednesday.

A trip to Radio Shack was all that was necessary. He chose the busiest one he could find, deep in the barrio in Santa Ana, and he deliberately took his time browsing until the youngest clerk with the most acne and the least amount of brainpower was available to wait on him. Then he made his purchase with cash: a call diverter, just the thing for those on-the-go SoCal folks who didn't want to miss an incoming phone call. No answering machine for those types. This would divert a phone call from one number to another by means of a simple computer chip. Once Douglas programmed the diverter with the number he wanted incoming calls diverted to, he would have an alibi for the night of his wife's murder. It was all so easy.

Donna had been a real numbskull to try to cheat on him. She had been a bigger numbskull to do her cheating on Wednesday nights because the fact of her doing it on Wednesday nights was what gave him the idea of how to snuff her. The volunteers on the hotline worked it in shifts. Generally there were two people present, each manning one of the telephone lines. But Newport Beach types actually didn't feel suicidal very often, and if they did, they were more likely to go to Neiman-Marcus and buy their way out of their depression. Midweek especially was a slow time for the pill-poppers and wrist-slashers, so the hotline was manned on Wednesdays by only one person a shift.

Douglas used the days prior to Wednesday to get his timing down to a military precision. He chose 8:30 as Donna's death hour, which would give him time to sneak out of the hotline office, drive home, put out her lights, and get back to the hotline before the next shift arrived at 9:00. He was carving it out fairly thin and allowing only a five minute margin of error, but he needed to do that in order to have a believable alibi once her body was found.

There could be neither noise nor blood, obviously. Noise would arouse the neighbours. Blood would damn him if he got so much as a drop on his clothes, DNA typing being what it is these days. So he chose his weapon carefully, aware of the irony of his choice. He would use the satin belt of one of her Victoria's Secret slay-him-where-he-stands dressing gowns. She had half a dozen, so he would remove one of them in advance of the murder, separate it from its belt, dispose of it in a dumpster behind the nearest Von's in advance of the killing – he liked that touch, getting rid of evidence *before* the crime, what killer ever thought of that? – and then use the belt to strangle his cheating wife on Wednesday night.

The call diverter would establish his alibi. He would take it to the suicide hotline, plug the phone into it, program the diverter with his cellular phone number, and thus appear to be in one location while his wife was being murdered in another. He made sure Donna was going to be at home by doing what he always did on Wednesdays: by phoning her from work before he left for the hotline.

'I feel like dogshit,' he told her at 5:40.

'Oh, Doug, no!' she replied. 'Are you ill or just feeling depressed about—'

'I'm feeling punk,' he interrupted her. The last thing he wanted was to listen to her phoney sympathy. 'It may have been lunch.'

'What did you have?'

Nothing. He hadn't eaten in two days. But he came up with, 'Shrimp', because he'd gotten food poisoning from shrimp a few years back and he thought she'd remember that, if she remembered anything at all about him at this point. He went on, 'I'm going to try to get home early from the hotline. I may not be able to if I can't pull in a substitute to take my shift. I'm heading over there now. If I can get a sub, I'll be home pretty early.'

He could hear her attempt to hide her dismay when she replied, 'But Doug . . . I mean, what time do you think you'll make it?'

'I don't know. By 8:00 at the latest, I hope. Why? What difference does it make?'

'No. None at all. But I thought you might like dinner . . .'

What she really thought was how she was going to have to cancel her hot romp with his baby brother. Douglas smiled at the realization of how nicely he'd just cooked her little caboose.

'Hell, I'm not hungry, Donna. I just want to go to bed if I can. You be there to rub my back? You going anywhere?'

'Of course not. Where would I be going? Doug, you sound strange. Is something wrong?'

Nothing was wrong, he told her. What he didn't tell her was how right everything was, felt, and was going to be. He had her where he wanted her now: she'd be home, and she'd be alone. She might phone Michael and tell him that his brother was coming home early so their tryst was off, but even if she did that, Michael's statement after her death would conflict with Douglas's uninterrupted presence at the suicide hotline that evening.

Douglas just had to make sure that he was back at the hotline with time to disassemble the call diverter. He'd get rid of it on the way home – nothing could be easier than flipping it into the trash behind the huge movie theatre complex that was on his route from the hotline to Harbour Heights where he lived – and then he'd arrive at his usual time of 9:20 to 'discover' the murder of his beloved.

It was all so easy. And so much cleaner and cheaper than divorcing the little whore.

He felt remarkably at peace, considering everything. He'd seen Thistle again and she'd held his Rolex, his wedding band, and his cuff links to take her reading. She'd greeted him by telling him that his aura was strong and that she could feel the power pulsing from him. And when she closed her eyes over his possessions, she'd said, 'I feel a major change coming into your life, Not-David. A change of location, perhaps, a change of climate. Are you taking a trip?'

He might be, he told her. He hadn't had a vacation in months. Did she have any suggested destinations?

'I see lights,' she responded, going her own way. 'I see cameras. I see many faces. You're surrounded by those you love.'

They would be at Donna's funeral, of course. And the press would cover it. He was somebody, after all. They wouldn't ignore the murder of Douglas Armstrong's wife. As for Thistle, she'd find out who he really was if she read the paper or watched the local news. But that made no difference since he'd never mentioned Donna and since he'd have an alibi for the time of her death.

He arrived at the suicide hotline at 5:56. He was relieving a UCI psych student named Debbie who was eager enough to be gone. She said, 'Only two calls, Mr Armstrong. If your shift is like mine, I hope you brought something to read.'

He waved his copy of *Money* magazine and took her place at the desk. He waited ten minutes after she'd left before he went out to his car to get the call diverter.

The hotline was located in the dock area of Newport, a maze of narrow one-way streets that traversed the top of Balboa Peninsula. By day, the streets' antique stores, marine chandleries, and second-hand clothing boutiques attracted both locals and tourists. By night, the place was a ghost town, uninhabited expect for the New Wave beatniks who visited a dive called the Omega Café three streets away, where anorexic girls dressed in black read poetry and strummed guitars. So no one was on the street to see Douglas fetch the call diverter from his Mercedes. And no one was on the street to see him leave the suicide hotline's small cubbyhole behind the real estate office at 8:15. And should any desperate individual call the hotline during his drive home, that call would be diverted onto his cellular phone and he could deal with it. God, the plan was perfect.

As he drove up the curving road that led to his house, Douglas thanked his stars that he'd chosen to live in an environment in which privacy was everything to the homeowners. Every estate sat, like Douglas's, behind walls and gates, shielded by trees. On one day in ten, he might actually see another resident. Most of the time – like tonight – there was no one around.

Even if someone had seen his Mercedes sliding up the hill, however, it was January dark and his was just another luxury vehicle in a community of Rolls-Royces, Bentleys, BMWs, Lexuses, Range Rovers, and other Mercedes. Besides, he'd already decided that if he saw someone or something suspicious, he would just turn around, go back to the hotline, and wait for another Wednesday.

But he didn't see anything out of the ordinary. He didn't see anyone. Perhaps a few more cars were parked on the street, but these were empty. He had the night to himself.

At the top of his drive, he shut off the engine and coasted to the house. It was dark inside, which told him that Donna was in the back, in their bedroom.

He needed her outside. The house was equipped with a security system that would do a bank vault proud, so he needed the killing to take place outside where a Peeping Tom gone bazooka or a burglar or a serial killer might have lured her. He thought of Ted Bundy and how he'd snagged his victims by appealing to their maternal need to come to his aid. He'd go the Bundy route, he decided. Donna was nothing if not eager to help.

He got out of the car silently and paced over to the door. He rang the bell with the back of his hand, the better to leave no trace on the button. In less than ten seconds, Donna's voice came over the intercom.

'Hi, babe,' he said. 'My hands are full. Can you let me in?'

'Be a sec,' she told him.

He took the satin belt from his pocket as he waited. He pictured her route from the back of the house. He twisted the satin round his hands and snapped it tight. Once she opened the door, he'd have to move like lightning. He'd have only one chance to fling the cord round her neck. The advantage he already possessed was surprise.

194

He heard her footsteps on the limestone. He gripped the satin and prepared. He thought of Michael. He thought of her together with Michael. He thought of his Asian erotica. He thought of betrayal, failure, and trust. She deserved this. They both deserved it. He was only sorry he couldn't kill Michael right now too.

When the door swung open, he heard her say, 'Doug! I thought you said—'

And then he was on her. He leapt. He yanked the belt round her neck. He dragged her swiftly out of the house. He tightened it and tightened it and tightened it and tightened it. She was too startled to fight back. In the five seconds it took her to get her hands to the belt in a reflex attempt to pull it away from her throat, he had it digging into her skin so deeply that her scrabbling fingers could find no slip of material to grab onto.

He felt her go limp. He said, 'Jesus. Yes. *Yes.*'

And then it happened.

The lights went on in the house. A Mariachi band started playing. People shouted 'Surprise! Surprise! Sur—'

Douglas looked up, panting, from the body of his wife, into popping flashes and a video camcorder. The joyous shouting from within his house was cut off by a single female shriek. He dropped Donna to the ground and stared without comprehension into the entry and, beyond that, the living room. There, at least three dozen people were gathered beneath a banner that said, 'Surprise, Dougie! Happy Five-Five!'

He saw the horrified faces of his brothers and their wives and children, of his own children, of his parents, of one of his former wives. And among them, his colleagues and his secretary. The chief of police. And the mayor.

He thought, What is this, Donna? Some kind of joke?

And then he saw Michael coming from the direction of the kitchen, Michael with a birthday cake in his hands, Michael calling out, 'Did we surprise him, Donna? Poor Doug. I hope his heart—' And then saying nothing at all when he saw his brother and his brother's wife.

Shit, Douglas thought. What have I done?

196

Which was, indeed, the question he'd be answering for the rest of his life.

Whet your appetite for murder with this taste of Elizabeth George's new bestseller, *In Pursuit of the Proper Sinner*, available now from Hodder & Stoughton.

It was just after seven the next morning when Julian returned to Maiden Hall. If he hadn't explored every possible site from Consall Wood to Alport Height, he certainly felt as if he had. Torch in one hand, loud hailer in the other, he'd gone through the motions: He'd trudged the leafy woodland path from Wettonmill up the steep grade to Thor's Cave. He'd scoured along the River Manifold. He'd shone his torchlight up the slope of Thorpe Cloud. He'd followed the River Dove as far south as the old medieval manor at Norbury. At the village of Alton, he'd hiked a distance along the Staffordshire Way. He'd driven as many as he could manage of the single lane roads that Nicola favoured. And he'd paused periodically to use the loud hailer in calling her name. Deliberately marking his presence in every location, he'd awakened sheep, farmers, and campers during his eight hours' search for her. At heart, he'd known there was no chance that he would find her, but at least he'd been *doing* something instead of waiting at home by the phone. At the end of it all, he felt anxious and empty. And completely fagged out, with throbbing eyeballs, bruised calves, and a back that ached from the night's exertion.

He was hungry as well. He could have eaten a leg of lamb had one been offered. It was odd, he thought. Just the previous night – wrought up with anticipation and nerves – he'd barely been able to touch his dinner. Indeed, Samantha had been a bit put out at the manner in which he merely picked at her fine sole amandine. She'd taken his lack of appetite personally, and while his father had leered about a man having other appetites to take care of, Sam, and wasn't their Julie about to do just that with we-all-know-who this very night, Samantha had pressed her lips together and cleared the table.

He'd have been able to do justice to one of her table-groaning breakfasts now, Julian thought. But as it was . . . Well, it didn't seem right to think about food – let alone to ask for it – despite the fact that the paying guests in Maiden Hall would be tucking into everything from corn flakes to kippers within the half hour.

He needn't have worried about the propriety in hoping for food under the circumstances, however. When he walked into the kitchen of Maiden Hall, a plate of scrambled eggs, mushrooms, and sausage sat untouched before Nan Maiden. She offered it to him the moment she saw him, saying, 'They want me to eat, but I can't. Please take it. I expect you could do with a meal.'

They were the early kitchen staff: two women from the nearby village of Grindleford who cooked in the mornings when the sophisticated culinary efforts of Christian-Louis were as unnecessary as they would be unwanted.

'Bring it with you, Julian.' Nan put a cafetiere on a tray with coffee mugs, milk, and sugar. She led the way into the dining room.

Only one table was occupied. Nan nodded at the couple who'd placed themselves in the bay window overlooking the garden and after politely inquiring about their night's sleep and their day's plans, she joined Julian at the table he'd chosen some distance away by the kitchen door.

The fact that she never wore make-up put Nan at a

disadvantage this morning. Her eyes were troughed by blue-grey flesh. Her skin, which was lightly freckled from time spent on her mountain bicycle when she had a free hour in which to exercise, was otherwise completely pallid. Her lips – having long ago lost the natural blush of youth – bore fine lines that began beneath her nose and were ghostly white. She hadn't slept; that much was clear.

She had, however, changed her clothes from the night before, apparently knowing that it would hardly do for the proprietress of Maiden Hall to greet her guests in the morning wearing what she'd worn as their hostess at dinner on the previous night. So her cocktail dress had been replaced by stirrup trousers and a tailored blouse.

She poured them each a cup of coffee and watched as Julian tucked into the eggs and mushrooms. She said, 'Tell me about the engagement. I need something to keep from thinking the worst.' When she spoke, tears caused her eyes to look glazed and unfocused, but she didn't weep.

Julian made himself mirror her control. 'Where's Andy?'

'Not back yet.' She circled her hands round her mug. Her grip was so tight that her fingers – their nails habitually bitten to the quick – were bleached of colour. 'Tell me about the two of you, Julian. Please. Tell me.'

'It's going to be all right,' Julian said. The last thing he wanted to force upon himself was having to concoct a scenario in which he and Nicola fell in love like ordinary human beings, realised that love, and founded upon it a life together. He couldn't face that at the moment. 'She's an experienced hiker. And she didn't go out there unprepared.'

'I know that. But I don't want to think about what it means that she hasn't come home. So tell me about the engagement. Where were you when you asked her? What did you say? What kind of wedding will it be? And when?'

Julian felt a chill at the double direction Nan's thoughts were taking. In either case, they brought up subjects he didn't want to consider. One led him to dwell upon the unthinkable. The other did nothing but encourage more lies.

He went for a truth that both of them knew. 'Nicola's been hiking in the Peaks since you moved from London. Even if she's hurt herself, she knows what to do till help arrives.' He forked up a portion of egg and mushrooms. 'It's lucky that she and I had a date. If we hadn't, God knows when we might've set out to find her.'

Nan looked away, but her eyes were still liquid. She lowered her head.

'We should be hopeful,' Julian went on. 'She's well-equipped. And she doesn't panic when things get dicey. We all know that.'

'But if she's fallen . . . or got lost in one of the caves . . . Julian, it happens. You know that. No matter how well prepared someone is, the worst still happens sometimes.'

'There's nothing that says anything's happened. I only looked in the south part of the White Peak. There're more square miles out there than can be covered by one man in total darkness in an evening. She could be anywhere. She could even have gone to the Dark Peak without our knowing.' He didn't mention the nightmare Mountain Rescue faced whenever someone *did* disappear in the Dark Peak. There was, after all, no mercy in fracturing Nan's tenuous hold on her calm. She knew the reality about the Dark Peak, anyway, and she didn't need him to point out to her that while roads made most of the White Peak accessible, its sister to the north could only be traversed by horseback, on foot, or by helicopter. If a hiker got lost or hurt up there, it generally took bloodhounds to find him.

'She said she'd marry you, though,' Nan declared, more to herself than to Julian, it seemed. 'She *did* say that she'd marry you, Julian?'

The poor woman seemed so eager to be lied to that Julian found himself just as eager to oblige her. 'We hadn't quite *got* to yes or no yet. That's what last night was supposed to be about.'

Nan lifted her coffee with both hands and drank. 'Was she . . . Did she seem pleased? I only ask because she'd seemed to have . . . Well, she'd seemed to have some sort of plans, and I'm not quite sure . . .'

Carefully Julian speared a mushroom. 'Plans?'

'I'd thought . . . Yes, it seemed so.'

He looked at Nan. Nan looked at him. He was the one to blink. He said steadily, 'Nicola had no plans that I know of, Nan.'

The kitchen door swung open a few inches. The face of one of the Grindleford women appeared in the aperture. She said, 'Mrs Maiden, Mr Britton,' in a low, hushed voice. And she used her head to indicate the direction of the kitchen. *You're wanted*, the motion implied.

Andy was leaning against one of the work tops, facing it, his weight on his hands and his head bowed. When his wife said his name, he looked up.

His face was drawn with exhaustion, and his growth of peppery whiskers fanned out from his moustache and shadowed his cheeks. His grey hair was uncombed, looking windblown although there wasn't any wind to speak of this morning. His eyes went to Nan, then slid away. Julian prepared himself to hear the worst.

'Her car's on the edge of Calder Moor,' Andy told them.

His wife drew her hands into a fist at her breast. 'Thank *God*,' she said.

Still, Andy didn't look at her. His expression indicated that thanks were premature. He knew what Julian knew and what Nan herself might well have acknowledged had she paused to probe for the possibilities that were indicated by the location of Nicola's Saab. Calder Moor was vast. It began just west of the road stretching between Blackwell and Brough, and it comprised endless expanses of heather and gorse, four caverns, numerous cairns and forts and barrows spanning time from Paleolithic through Iron Age, gritstone outcroppings and limestone caves and fissures through which more than one foolish tripper had crawled for adventure and become hopelessly stuck. Julian knew that Andy was thinking of this as he stood in the kitchen at the end of his long night's search for Nicola. But Andy was thinking something else as well. Andy was *knowing* something else, in fact. That much was evident from the manner in which he straightened and began slapping the knuckles of one hand against the heel of the other.

Julian said, 'Andy, for God's sake, *tell* us.'

Andy's gaze fixed on his wife. 'The car's not on the verge, like you'd think it should be.'

'Then where . . . ?'

'It's out of sight behind a wall, on the road out of Sparrowpit.'

'But that's good, isn't it?' Nan said eagerly. 'If she went

camping, she wouldn't want to leave the Saab on the road. Not where it could be seen by someone who might break into it.'

'True,' he said. 'But the car's not alone.' And with a glance towards Julian as if he wished to apologise for something, 'There's a motorcycle with it.'

'Someone out for a hike,' Julian said.

'At this hour?' Andy shook his head. 'It was wet from the night. As wet as her car. It's been there just as long.'

Nan eagerly said, 'Then she didn't go onto the moor alone? She met someone there?'

'Or she was followed,' Julian added quietly.

'I'm calling the police,' Andy said. 'They'll want to bring in Mountain Rescue now.'

When a patient died, it was Phoebe Neill's habit to turn to the land for comfort. She generally did this alone. She'd lived alone for most of her life, and she wasn't afraid of solitude. And in the combination of solitude and a return to the land, she received consolation. When she was out in nature, nothing manmade stood between her and the Great Creator. Thus on the land, she was able to align herself with the end of a life and the will of God, knowing that the body we inhabit is but a shell that binds us for a period of temporal experience prior to our entering the world of the spirit for the next phase of our development.

This Thursday morning things were different, though. Yes, a patient had died on the previous evening. Yes, Phoebe Neill turned to the land for solace. But on this occasion, she hadn't come alone. She'd brought with her a mixed breed dog of uncertain lineage, the now-orphaned pet of the young man whose life had just ended.

She'd been the one to talk Stephen Fairbrook into getting a dog as a companion during the last year of his illness. So when it had become clear that the end of Stephen's life was fast approaching, she knew that she'd make his passing easier if she reassured him about the dog's fate. 'Stevie, when the time comes, I'm happy to take Benbow,' she'd told him one morning as she bathed his skeletal body and massaged lotion into his shrunken limbs. 'You're not to worry about him. All right?'

You can die now was what went unspoken. Not because words like *die* or *death* were unmentionable round Stephen Fairbrook, but because once he'd been told his disease, been through countless treatments and drugs in an effort to stay alive long enough for a cure to be found, watched his weight decline and his hair fall out and his skin bloom with bruises that turned into sores, *die* and *death* were old companions to him. He didn't need a formal introduction to guests who were already dwelling within his house.

On the last afternoon of his master's life Benbow had known Stephen was passing. And hour after hour, the animal lay quietly next to him, moving only if Stephen moved, his muzzle resting in Stephen's hand until Stephen had left them. Benbow, in fact, had known before Phoebe that Stephen was gone. He'd risen, whimpered, howled once, and was silent. He'd then sought out the comfort of his basket, where he'd stayed until Phoebe had collected him.

Now he raised himself on his hind legs, his plumed tail wagging hopefully as Phoebe parked her car in a lay-by near a drystone wall and reached for his lead. He barked once. Phoebe smiled. 'Yes. A walk shall make us right as rain, old chap.'

She clambered out. Benbow followed, leaping agilely from the Vauxhall and sniffing eagerly, nose pressed to the sandy ground like a canine Hoover. He led Phoebe directly to the wall and snuffled along it until he came to the stile that would allow him access to the moor beyond. This he leapt over easily, and once on the other side he paused to shake himself off. His ears pricked up and he cocked his head. He gave a sharp bark to tell Phoebe that a solo run, not a walk on a lead, was what he had in mind.

'Can't do it, old boy,' Phoebe told him. 'Not till we see what's what and who's who on the moor, all right?' She was cautious and overprotective that way, which made for excellent skills when it came to nursing the house-bound dying through their final days, particularly those whose conditions required hyper-vigilance on the part of their care giver. But when it came to children or to dog ownership, Phoebe knew intuitively that the natural hovering born of a cautious nature would have produced a fearful animal or a rebellious child. So she'd had no child – although she'd had her opportunities – and she'd had no dog till now. 'I hope to do right by you, Benbow,' she told the mongrel. He lifted his head to look at her, past the scraggly kelp-coloured mop of fur that flopped into his eyes. He swung back round towards the open moor, mile after mile of heather creating a purple shawl that covered the shoulders of the land.

Had the moor consisted of heather alone, Phoebe would not have given a second thought to letting Benbow have his romp unrestrained. But the seemingly endless flow of the heather was deceptive to the uninitiated. Ancient limestone quarries produced unexpected lacunae in the landscape, into which the dog could tumble, and the caverns, lead mines, and caves into which he could scamper – and where she could not follow – served as a siren enticement for any animal, an enticement with which Phoebe Neill didn't care to compete. But she was willing to let Benbow snuffle freely through one of the many birch copses that grew in irregular clumps on the moor, rising like feathers against the sky, and she grasped his lead firmly and began heading northwest where the largest of the copses grew.

It was a fine morning, but there were no other walkers about yet. The sun was low in the eastern sky, and Phoebe's shadow stretched far to her left as if it wished to pursue a cobalt horizon that was heaped with clouds so white they might have been giant sleeping swans. There was little wind, just enough of a breeze to slap Phoebe's windcheater against her sides and flip Benbow's tangled fur from his eyes. There was no scent on this breeze that Phoebe could discern. And the only noise came from an unkindness of ravens somewhere on the moor and a flock of sheep bleating in the distance.

Benbow snuffled along, investigating nasally every inch of the path as well as the mounds of heather that edged it. He was a cooperative walker, as Phoebe had discovered from the thrice-daily strolls she and he had taken once Stephen had been completely confined to bed. And because she didn't have to tug him along or pull him back or encourage the little dog in any way, their jaunt on the moor gave her time to pray.

She didn't pray for Stephen Fairbrook. She knew that Stephen was now at peace, quite beyond the necessity of an intervention – Divine or otherwise – in the process of the inevitable. What she prayed for was greater understanding. She wanted to know why a scourge had come to dwell among them, felling the best, the brightest, and frequently those with the most to offer. She wanted to know what conclusion she was meant to draw from the deaths of young men who were guilty of nothing, of the deaths of children whose crime was to be born of infected mothers, and of the deaths of those unfortunate mothers as well.

When Benbow wanted to pick up the pace, she was willing to do so. In this manner, they strode into the heart of the moor, ambling along one path, forking off onto another. Phoebe wasn't worried about becoming lost. She knew that they'd begun their walk southeast of a limestone outcrop that was called Agricola's Throne. It was the remains of a great Roman fort, a windswept outlook shaped not unlike an enormous chair that marked the edge of the moor. It towered above a valley of pastures, villages, and derelict mills, and anyone sighting off the throne during a hike was unlikely to get lost.

They'd been trekking for an hour when Benbow's ears pricked up and his stance altered. From shuffling along happily, he came to a sudden halt. His body elongated, back legs stretching out. His feathery tail stiffened into an immobile quill. A low whine issued from his throat.

Phoebe studied what lay before them: the copse of birches she'd intended to allow Benbow to gambol in. 'Gracious me,' she murmured. 'Aren't you the clever one, Bennie?' She was deeply surprised and just as deeply touched

211

by the mongrel's ability to read her intentions. She'd silently promised him freedom when they reached the copse. And here the copse was. He read her mind and was eager to be off the lead. 'Can't blame you a bit,' Phoebe said as she knelt to unhook the lead from his collar. She wound the rope of braided leather round her hand and rose with a grunt as the dog shot ahead of her into the trees.

Phoebe walked after him, smiling at the sight of his compact body bouncing along the path. He used his feet like springs as he ran, bounding off the ground with all four legs at once as if it were his intention to fly. He skirted a large column of roughly hewn lime-stone on the edge of the copse and vanished among the birches.

This was the entrance to Nine Sisters' Henge, a Neolithic earth-banked enclosure that encircled nine standing stones of varying heights. Assembled some thirty-five hundred years before the time of Christ, the henge and the stones marked a spot for rituals engaged in by prehistoric man. At the time of its use, the henge had been standing in open land that had been cleared of its natural oak and alder forest. Now, however, it was hidden from view, buried within a thick growth of birches, a modern encroachment on the resulting moorland.

Phoebe paused and surveyed her surroundings. The eastern sky – without the clouds of the west – allowed the sun to pierce unimpeded through the trees. Their bark was the white of a seagull's wing, but patterned with diamond-shaped cracks the colour of coffee. Leaves formed a shimmering green screen in the morning breeze, which served to shield the ancient stone circle within the copse from an inexperienced hiker who didn't know it was there. Standing before the birches, the sentry stone was hit by the light at an oblique angle. This deepened its natural pocking, and from a distance the shadows combined to effect a face, an austere custodian of secrets too ancient to be imagined.

As Phoebe observed the stone, an unaccountable chill passed through her. Despite the breeze, it was silent here. No noise from the dog, no bleating of a sheep lost among the stones, no call of hikers as they crossed the moor. It was altogether too silent, Phoebe thought. And she found herself glancing round uneasily, overcome by the feeling that she was being watched.

Phoebe thought herself a practical woman, one not given to casual fancies or an imagination run riot with ghosties and ghoulies and things that go bump in the night. Nonetheless, she felt the sudden need to be away from this place, and she called for the dog. There was no response.

'Benbow!' she called a second time. 'Here, boy. *Come*.'

Nothing. The silence intensified. The breeze stilled. And Phoebe felt the hair stirring on the back of her neck.

She didn't wish to approach the copse, but she didn't know why. She'd walked among the Nine Sisters before. She'd even had a quiet picnic lunch there one fine spring day. But there was something about the place this morning . . .

A sharp bark from Benbow and suddenly what seemed like hundreds of ravens took to the air in an ebony swarm. For a moment they entirely blocked out the sun. The shadow they cast seemed like a monstrous fist sweeping over Phoebe. She shuddered at the distinct sensation of

213

having been marked somehow, like Cain before being sent to the east.

She swallowed and turned back to the copse. There was no further sound from Benbow, no response to her calling. Concerned, Phoebe hurried along the path, passed the limestone guardian of that sacred place, and entered the trees.

They grew thickly, but visitors to the site had trod a path through them over the years. On this, the natural grass of the moor had been flattened and worn through to the earth in spots. To the sides, however, bilberry bushes formed part of the undergrowth, and the last of the wild purple orchids gave off their characteristic scent of cats in the tough moor grass. It was here beneath the trees that Phoebe looked for Benbow, drawing nearer to the ancient stones. The silence round her was so profound that the very fact of it seemed like an augur, mute but eloquent all at once.

Then, as Phoebe drew near the circle's boundary, she finally heard the dog again. He yelped from somewhere, then emitted something between a whine and a growl. It was decidedly fearful. Worried that he'd encountered a hiker who was less than welcoming of his canine advances, Phoebe hastened towards the sound, through the remaining trees and into the circle.

At once, she saw a mound of bright blue at the inner base of one of the standing stones. It was at this mound that Benbow barked, backing off from it now with his hackles up and his ears flattened back against his skull.

'What is it?' Phoebe asked, over his noise. 'What've you found, old boy?' Uneasily, she wiped her palms on her skirt and glanced about. She saw the answer to her question lying round her. What the dog had found was a scene of chaos. The centre of the stone circle was strewn with white feathers, and the detritus of some thoughtless campers lay scattered about: everything from a tent to a cooking pot to an opened rucksack spilling its contents onto the ground.

Phoebe approached the dog through this clutter. She wanted to get Benbow back on the lead and get both of them out of the circle at once.

She said, 'Benbow, come here,' and he yelped more loudly. It was the sort of sound she'd never heard from him before.

She saw that he was clearly upset by the mound of blue, the source of the white feathers that dusted the clearing like the wings of slaughtered moths.

It was a sleeping bag, she realised. And it was from this bag that the feathers had come, because a slash in the nylon that served as its cover spat more white feathers when Phoebe touched the bag with her toe. Indeed, nearly all the feathers that constituted its stuffing were gone. What remained was like a tarpaulin. It had been completely unzipped and it was shrouding something, something that terrified the little dog.

Phoebe felt weak-kneed, but she made herself do it. She lifted the cover. Benbow backed off, giving her a clear look at the nightmare vignette that the sleeping bag had covered.

Blood. There was more in front of her than she'd ever seen before. It wasn't bright red because it had obviously been exposed to air for a good number of hours. But Phoebe didn't require that colour to know what she was looking at.

'Oh my Lord.' She went light-headed.

She'd seen death before in many guises, but none had been as grisly as this. At her feet, a young man lay curled like a foetus, dressed head-to-toe in nothing but black, with that same colour puckering burnt flesh from eye to jaw on one side of his face. His cropped hair was black as well, as was the pony tail that sprang from his skull. His goatee was black. His fingernails were black. He wore an onyx ring and an earring of black. The only colour that offered relief from the black – aside from the sleeping bag of blue – was the magenta of blood, and that was everywhere: on the ground beneath him, saturating his clothes, pooling from scores of wounds on his torso.

Phoebe dropped the sleeping bag and backed away from the body. She felt hot. She felt cold. She knew that she was about to faint. She chided herself for her lack of backbone. She said, 'Benbow?' and over her voice, she heard the dog barking. She realised that he'd never stopped. But four of her senses had deadened with shock, heightening and honing her fifth sense: sight.

She scooped up the dog and stumbled from the horror.